"What is the line you intend to take with my niece?"

Angela schooled her expression into revealing nothing but the professionalism of someone paid to do a job.

"Natasha needs very careful, gentle handling. Was she a happy child before...before the accident?"

Nick's eyes narrowed. "Isn't that something you would know? Considering you were in close contact with my sister? Why wouldn't she have told you if she was having difficulties with Natasha?"

"Perhaps she didn't like to mention problems, considering that Natasha was adopted."

He let that one go, but Angela would have to watch her step more carefully. It was a shame, because she really would have liked to ask whether Natasha had ever expressed curiosity about her natural mother, about *her*...

CATHY WILLIAMS is Trinidadian and was brought up on the twin islands of Trinidad and Tobago. She was awarded a scholarship to study in Britain, and went to Exeter University in 1975 to continue her studies into the great loves of her life: languages and literature. It was there that Cathy met her husband, Richard. Since they married, Cathy has lived in England, originally in the Thames Valley but now in the Midlands. Cathy and Richard have three small daughters.

Books by Cathy Williams

HARLEQUIN PRESENTS®

1413—A POWERFUL ATTRACTION
1502—CARIBBEAN DESIRE
1829—BEYOND ALL REASON
1993—A DAUGHTER FOR CHRISTMAS
2006—A SUITABLE MISTRESS
2048—THE BABY VERDICT

CATHY WILLIAMS

A Natural Mother

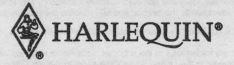

HARLEQUIN®

TORONTO • NEW YORK • LONDON
AMSTERDAM • PARIS • SYDNEY • HAMBURG
STOCKHOLM • ATHENS • TOKYO • MILAN • MADRID
PRAGUE • WARSAW • BUDAPEST • AUCKLAND

ISBN 0-373-12076-1

A NATURAL MOTHER

First North American Publication 2000.

PROLOGUE

SHE had had nine long, agonised months to think about this, and thought about it she had. Every angle, every nuance, every turning and corner and nook and cranny. And she had told herself, over and over again, that this was the best way. The only way. But now that the time had finally arrived, in the blink of an eye or so it seemed, Angela found that she was gripping the side of the bed, steeling herself so that she didn't break down and weep. Her body felt as rigid as a piece of board.

The hospital room was very small. It held a bed—one of those typically narrow, uncomfortable beds that didn't allow for much movement—a wardrobe, and a chair which was propped by the window. There was an *en suite* bathroom as well. Luxury, really, but a private room was something that the Streetmans had insisted on. Angela had insisted on meeting them from the moment she had made her mind up, and they had fussed over her from the first. In a few minutes they would come in. They would be glowing with delight, alive with happiness. So one door would shut and another would open.

The social worker was talking to her, gently and kindly, and Angela let the reassuring monotone of her words wash over her. She was finding it difficult to think, to move. Her whole body ached with the effort of keeping her emotions in check. She would have liked to scream, to take what was hers and rush out of that hospital room with its antiseptic smell. She had to remind herself that she had nothing to rush *to*.

She glanced into the small, square mirror stuck onto the wardrobe door, and repeated the same old refrain that she had repeated to herself so many times over the past few months.

She was seventeen, just. She had no siblings, no mother she could turn to. Her father didn't want her. The bottle was the only companion he had needed from as far back as she could remember.

What kind of life was that for a baby?

The reflection in the mirror grew blurry and she blinked rapidly a few times. She didn't dare look at the baby any more. She couldn't afford to bond. That was something that the social worker had told her. Best to let go, to think about what was right for the baby. The Streetmans were warm, caring people. They would be able to give her baby everything that she couldn't. And they had promised to keep in touch, to send pictures, to maintain a link, and she believed them.

She couldn't look at the small miracle of life lying there, with its mop of dark hair, but she reached out to the small plastic cot by the side of the bed and groped until she found her daughter's hand, and she held it and told herself that, yes, she was doing the right thing.

CHAPTER ONE

THE taxi driver dropped her off outside the house. He had talked incessantly on the way from the station, and Angela had dutifully murmured what she hoped were the right responses, but she had felt ill with nerves and now, staring at the daunting façade of the house, she was beginning to feel even more ill, if that was possible.

She hoped desperately that none of it showed on her face. She had waited almost a year for this opportunity, and she wasn't about to let the sickening wrench in her stomach ruin it for her. Nick Cameron would never employ a potential neurotic to look after his niece.

I am twenty-five years old, she told herself firmly, a trained schoolteacher, and I am fairly presentable. She smoothed down her skirt, a businesslike shade of grey with a matching short-sleeved jacket, bought especially because she thought that she needed the right ensemble if she was to create the right impression. Her shoulder-length blonde hair had been curled into a bun at the nape of her neck. It felt awkward, because she was so accustomed to wearing it loose or else in a ponytail, and she nervously smoothed her hands over that too, making sure that stray bits hadn't escaped.

'Oh, dear Lord,' she whispered to herself, 'please let me make the right impression.' She blocked out from her mind the sheer intensity of her need for this job. She refused to think beyond the moment.

If only, she thought to herself, the house wasn't so *big*. She hadn't thought that houses in London were ever this enormous. It was a great big Victorian mansion, set back from the road, with chimneys and bay windows. The gardens didn't run to acres, but they were substantial by London standards. Enough to leave her in no doubt of the owner's considerable wealth.

She wished that she knew more about him. What was he like as a person? What did he look like? How old was he? Any scrap of knowledge might have allayed some of the paralysing fear rushing through her, but the Streetmans, dutiful as they had been in communicating with her, sending her photos of her daughter as each birthday crept past and the long, hard months flowed into years, had never once spoken about anything or anyone other than Natasha.

She pressed the doorbell and waited, and was finally rewarded with the muffled sounds of movement.

Her stomach tensed in preparation, then she let out a sigh of relief when the door was opened by a middle-aged woman, who glanced at her briefly and stated rather than asked, 'You must be Miss Field.'

Angela was almost tempted to reply, Yes, I know, but instead she smiled and nodded and allowed herself to be ushered into the large hall.

'Mr Cameron is waiting for you in his study,' the woman said, shutting the door and heading down the hall, while Angela followed in her wake, clutching her bag with both hands in front of her.

Her instant impression of the house was one of immense space and a great deal of taste. The hall was papered in pale colours, and there was a trio of impressive paintings on one side, hung, not in the orthodox manner, but from thin, gold chains which were hooked from picture rails. An oak-banistered staircase hooked off from the right, but they ignored this, as they did all of the rooms on the ground floor, glimpsed through half opened doors.

The middle-aged woman was as reticent as the taxi driver had been garrulous. She led the way through a large yellow room, which appeared to be some kind of secondary dining area, down a step into the kitchen, then through three utility and storage rooms decorated with the sort of impeccable finish which most people would have envied for their best rooms.

It was a house to linger over. It had the graceful, attractive dimensions of all Victorian houses—high ceilings, a feeling of solidity. However, not only were they not lingering, but now that they were standing in front of the door which obviously led to the study in question Angela could no longer even appreciate her fleeting, superficial impressions of the place. Everything around her seemed to have been suddenly blotted out. All she could see was the housekeeper in front of her and the stripped pine door with the old-fashioned latch above the handle.

All she could think was that on that day in March, over eight years ago, her life had taken a turning of monumental importance. Now, here, it was about to do the same again. If luck was on her side.

She heard a man's deep voice say 'Yes!' in response to the housekeeper's knock on the door, then her body took over and did what was necessary to get from A to B. Her mind might well have been frozen, but her feet, thank God, still moved. Her mouth still uttered a thank you to the housekeeper, which met with a nod and her first smile since Angela had entered the house, her jaws unlocked from their rigidity and she entered the room and braced herself to meet Nick Cameron.

She had had no idea what to expect. Amanda Streetman had been a tall, fair-haired, attractive woman with a face that had lent itself readily to smiles. She had been sophisticated, but not alarmingly so. Had she been alive, she would have been in her early forties now. Angela had no real inkling what she would have looked like, apart from the image her imagination threw up, because the regular annual photos had always been of Natasha alone, without either parent in the background, or else, if they were there, they were on the edge of the picture, an indistinct image.

Nick Cameron bore no resemblance to his sister, apart from the same perfect bone structure.

She stood, poised in the doorway, and stared at the man who had swivelled around in his leather chair to look at her.

He was as dark as his sister had been fair. Dark hair, grey eyes, the sort of aggressively masculine face that made most women stop in their tracks and take a second look.

'Miss Field,' he drawled. 'So we meet at last. Please come in. There's no need to stand there as though you're about to take flight. I won't eat you.'

He should have smiled jovially when he said this, a warm smile that would have put her at her ease, but he didn't. Her immediate impression was not of a man who handed out jovial smiles indiscriminately. He watched, she thought uncomfortably, he assessed, he reached his silent conclusions.

The grey eyes were sharp, intense, the sort of eyes that appeared to see everything. What would he see in her if he looked too hard? The answer to that was frightening enough to shake her out of her momentary lapse of concentration, and she walked into the room and sat down in the chair facing his.

'Would you like something to drink, Miss Field?' he asked. 'Tea? Coffee?' He crossed his legs, a lazy movement that made her suspect that he was a man who was fully aware of his own powerful appeal, whether or not he used the information to his advantage.

Angela shook her head and managed a smile.

'Thank you, but no. I've had rather a lot of coffee today already. On the train down to London.'

'Fine. We'll get down to business, then, shall we?'

She wished that he didn't make her so nervous. She was clutching her bag. Again. She forced her fingers to relax.

'I won't pretend that I wasn't curious when I received your letter out of the blue four months ago.' The letter in question was lying on the desk next to him and he picked it up and scanned it, as if reminding himself of the contents.

'I can understand that—' Angela began. There were certain questions which she had prepared herself for, and this was one of them, but he interrupted her before she could launch into her carefully worked out explanation.

'Of course, my contact with Mandy was limited, unfortunately, because we lived in different countries, but I never once heard her mention your name, even in passing.'

There was enough speculation in the silver-grey eyes to send another shiver racing down Angela's spine, but she smiled again, and said, 'Perhaps you've forgotten.'

'I rarely forget anything, Miss Field.' For a second he looked slightly amused at the thought that he could ever find himself guilty of that particular human failing. 'Nor does Natasha remember your name being mentioned in any context whatsoever. A strange sort of friendship you must have had with my sister.'

This time there was a question there, lurking behind the flat statement.

'Only in so far as we didn't meet very often. We spoke on the phone fairly regularly and we also communicated by letter.' The phone bit was a generous elaboration of the truth, but the letter bit, at least, was true—though not in the way he would have interpreted it.

Their eyes met and she felt another ripple of something, some sensation that was a mixture of apprehension and fascination. She couldn't remember a time when she had felt so uneasily *aware* of a man's presence. Once she had fallen for a charm she had thought sincere, and she had paid a heavy price for her mistake. Since then she had put her emotions into cold storage and shut the door on them. It had been easy. The repercussions of her poor judgement had seen to that.

'Yet, you didn't attend the funeral.'

'I'm afraid not.' She refused to be drawn into anything that could lead her away from the plotted path. It didn't take a genius with the IQ of Einstein to recognise that Nick Cameron was a man who could elicit the answers that he wanted through any number of devious means—and any inconsistencies in those answers would not be swept under the carpet and forgotten. Hadn't he already told her that he forgot nothing?

'Tell me how you met Mandy,' he said abruptly, as though the subject of the funeral was one which he, too, was more than happy to leave alone.

Angela relaxed a little. 'I was at school still,' she said. 'Just seventeen.' Her voice faded a bit at that, and she made an effort to carry on in a brisker manner. 'Studying art. Your sister came to give a lecture to us on Chagall

and while she was there she had a look around at some
of the drawings we had done. Some still life. A few land-
scapes.'

There was enough truth interweaving with the fabri-
cation to give a certain believable body to what she was
saying. She *had* been studying art at school when she'd
become pregnant. Art and English. Amanda Streetman
had not come to give a talk, but she'd used to do those
things at that time. It was one of the snippets of information that Angela had gleaned over the months of her
pregnancy, when they had been in contact. In fact, she
had looked at several of Angela's paintings and had been
impressed.

'She was always very interested in new talent,' Nick
agreed expressionlessly.

'I'm so very sorry,' she said impulsively, leaning forward. 'I was devastated when I learned of the accident.'
A dark, rainy night... The Streetmans travelling back
from a dinner party somewhere... Their car had lost control round a bend. She had only unearthed those scant
facts months after the event, and only after a great deal
of searching.

'Thank you,' Nick said, with a harsh frown, and she
wondered whether she had overstepped a mark somewhere. 'So she kept in touch, did she?'

'Yes.' She looked down at her fingers, lightly entwined
on the bag on her lap. 'That was how I knew of Natasha.'
She could hardly bring herself to look at him when she
said that. She was afraid of what he would see in her
eyes. Perhaps a flicker of expression that might not quite
fit in with the detached story she was telling. 'She was
very proud of Natasha. She said that she loved art.' That
was pure speculation. Dangerous ground. But didn't all

children like drawing and painting? It would be more unusual if she hated it.

'Yes, she appears to.' He paused, and then said bluntly, 'You know the circumstances behind her?' He looked at her very carefully, waiting for her response, and Angela wondered whether this was a trick question. It irked her even though she could see the reasoning behind it.

The Streetmans had been well off. He, himself, from all appearances, had more money at his disposal than he probably knew what to do with. It must strike him as odd that from nowhere he had received a letter from a woman he had never met in his life before, who claimed to be a friend of his deceased sister even though no one appeared ever to have heard of her. A letter in which she was suggesting herself for a job looking after a child she had clearly never met in her life before, and that said she was prepared to travel to America if needs be.

Thinking about it, she was surprised that he had not tossed it into the wastepaper basket without a second glance, and that now, having agreed to interview her, he had not sat her down with a questionnaire full of trick questions.

'She's adopted. Yes, I know.' Her voice was perfectly devoid of expression.

'My sister couldn't have children.'

'She had a ruptured appendix when she was eight years old and it completely destroyed her reproductive system. I know.'

He looked at her for a long time. She could see him thinking; she could almost *hear* him thinking. But she had no idea what.

He stood up and sauntered towards the window, which overlooked a conservatory and, beyond, the well-tended garden.

Angela followed him with her eyes, and again felt that strange, disturbing awareness—a jumbled awareness of him as a possible threat, as a man, as someone to step lightly around, the way you might step around an animal that had the potential to destroy.

There was something ever so slightly untamed and dangerous about the way he looked. Good looks honed into something dark and aggressive. A face that suggested power, formidable self-control, frightening intelligence. A body that was hard and athletic. She wondered how he would react if he ever discovered the real reason behind her sudden appearance in his life, and she dismissed the thought quickly.

'Not many people know that,' he said, turning to face her, so that the sun, streaming in from behind him, made it difficult for her to see his expression properly. 'I find it hard to believe that she knew you well enough to confide that fact to you, yet to all intents and purposes you played no part in her social life.'

Angela didn't say anything. Put like that, it certainly sounded pretty odd indeed, and she couldn't think of any reason she could come up with that wouldn't sound feeble and contrived.

'I also find it a little strange that she never felt any inclination to introduce you to Natasha, even though she was obviously close enough to you to make you her confidante on matters only a handful of people were aware of.'

'She sent me pictures,' Angela said on a sigh. There could have been no contact between the two of them. She had always relied on Natasha making her way back when she was old enough, when she was ready to find out *why*.

'Something here doesn't seem to tie up,' he said. 'Wouldn't you agree?'

'No.' Angela looked at him full in the eyes. 'It all seems perfectly crystal-clear to me.'

'Perhaps my logical mind is failing me here, then,' he continued, and she could feel him circling her, probing her for an explanation that was currently beyond his grasp.

'Perhaps it is,' Angela said calmly. She was sitting upright in the chair, her hands primly folded on her lap, her eyes clear and bland. 'Perhaps you should see your doctor about it.'

For the first time he looked genuinely amused. He flashed her a brief smile and it occurred to her, as colour rushed into her face, that there was something else she had failed to see. Charm. The promise of sensuality underneath the hard exterior.

Really not her type at all. What a shame Amanda Streetman's brother hadn't been more run of the mill.

'How did you find out what had happened?' he asked curiously. He sat back slightly, against the window ledge, and crossed his arms.

She wished that he would sit down. In her constant effort to look up at him, some of her hair had escaped its stranglehold of clips and she pushed the stray bits behind her ears.

'You look too young for a bun,' he remarked casually. She saw his eyes appraise her momentarily, and her mouth tightened.

'I normally wear it loose,' she replied, with an attempt to sound as casual as he had.

'But you decided to go for the tried and tested school-teacher hairstyle to make a good impression.'

'Of course not!' Angela snapped, only afterwards remembering that that was precisely what she had done, and that snapping at her potential employer wasn't such a great idea. 'I'm twenty-five years old,' she added, apropos of nothing. 'And I *am* a schoolteacher.'

'Yes, well, we shall get to that in a minute. Now, tell me how you discovered what had happened.' He pushed himself away from the window ledge and strolled towards the door, which made her wonder whether she was expected to proffer her explanation to a vanishing back. But he simply yelled to the housekeeper, who was in the kitchen, to bring them in some tea.

'Eva's hard of hearing,' he explained, sitting back down. 'Now, where were we?'

'How I discovered what had happened.' Why did he pretend that he had lost track of the conversation? There was no way this man lost track of anything. He would probably be able to reproduce the entire conversation between them, word for word, weeks after it had taken place.

'Carry on.'

'I had tried getting in touch with your sister.' No word, no birthday photo. Weeks of living in a state of suppressed anxiety wondering what was going on. 'Finally, I made some enquiries.'

'Why didn't you just drive down?' His mild voice didn't fool her for an instant. He was still perplexed by her and was still trying to catch her out.

'I was particularly busy at school, and anyway, I have no car. I decided to telephone Natasha's school instead and find out what was going on. A simple phone call seemed easier than trying to fit a complicated trip into a fairly hectic diary.'

Did that sound as weak to him as it did to her? She had made it sound as though she had known where

Natasha had gone to school, but in fact that too had required a fair bit of detective work. She had telephoned every private school within a certain area and had finally hit on the right one. Getting the information had not been difficult. Perhaps it had helped that it had been a matter of one schoolteacher speaking to another.

'And on the spur of the moment you decided to write to me, in New York, and offer your services as a nanny of sorts. Abandoning your well-paid job in the process, and solely because of an empathy based on a few photos my sister had sent you over the years.'

'I admit it sounds a little bizarre.'

Eva's appearance with a tray laden with cups, saucers, teapot, jug of milk, sugar and a plate of shortbread, all balanced in a fairly cavalier fashion, couldn't have come at a better time. It gave Angela time to gather her thoughts together. She would have to sound convincing. The wealthy were suspicious by nature, and she couldn't afford to arouse his suspicions, whatever direction they took.

'The fact is...' She took a deep breath. What *was* the fact? 'The fact is that I have been toying with the idea of giving up my teaching for a while now. I studied Fine Art at university and yet here I am, teaching art to fourteen-year-olds at a secondary school.'

She paused and waited until tea had been poured, then she took her cup and sipped from it, trying to look convincingly thoughtful on the subject and not nervously aware that the man sitting opposite her was unsettling her in a way she could not have imagined possible.

'There is no way that I can devote any time to my painting, not while I hold down a full-time job as well.'

'What about the holidays.'

What *about* them? she wanted to snap. Why did he have to grill her?

'Quite a bit is accounted for with school duties. In the summer holidays I always help out with summer school for a few weeks. Then there's always preparation for the term ahead. I don't know whether I would have done anything about it, but I suppose when I heard about your sister and realised that Natasha had been left without parents and transported to America to live, the thought occurred to me that we might both help one another. I might be able to find some time to paint and I thought that she might be lonely out there, appreciative of an English face—especially of someone who knew her mother.'

How desperately she had waited for a reply to that letter. Every day rushing through the front door after school, gathering the letters from the mat. Days and weeks of disappointment when nothing from America lay waiting for her. She had almost given up, and was considering the financial implications of using her savings so that she could travel to New York and simply show up on his doorstep, when his letter had finally arrived.

'And you don't think that you might find it a little undemanding moving from a job involving a class full of children to one child.'

Never. Not when that one child is my daughter. 'Might I be permitted to ask a question?' she said aloud.

He raised his eyebrows, as though a little amused at the antiquated phrasing of the question. 'Go ahead, Miss Field. After all, interviews are a two-way business. I expect that there is more than one question you'd like to ask me.' He settled back in his chair and stared at her lazily.

'What brings you to London?'

'A move I've been considering for quite a while now.

My businesses in American are thriving. They're more
or less well-oiled enough to carry on smoothly without
any intervention from me—or rather minimal intervention. Natasha's arrival...' He paused and frowned, as
though trying to work out carefully what he would say
next. 'My niece's arrival precipitated the decision.' He
stood up and walked restlessly around the room, his
hands stuck into his pockets.

Angela watched him in silence, waiting for him to
carry on. For a man as tall as he was, he moved with a
peculiar lithe grace. She wondered, in passing, why she
was paying so much attention to Nick Cameron's physical attributes. Not just because she was in the middle of
a very stressful interview, the results of which would
have far-reaching complications for her and for Natasha,
but also because she never speculated on men in the same
way that other women appeared to. Lessons learnt the
hard way were never forgotten.

She decided to put it down to the fact that she was
here, in this office with him, under strange circumstances,
to say the least. The adrenaline was running through her,
changing her normal responses, sensitising her to things
to which she was normally immune.

Also, and this she admitted somewhat more reluctantly, he *was* an outstanding man, at least from the physical point of view, and she *was*, after all, cooped up with
him in a very confined space. It would have been hard
not to focus on him in a fairly thorough way.

She stopped looking at him and resumed quiet contem-
plation of her hands.

'You seem to have known my sister rather well, despite a puzzling lack of social contact, so you must have
known how...' He paused again and she could sense him
struggling to find the right words. 'How close a family

they were. Natasha was very attached to both my sister and her husband, and because she was adopted, and an only child at that, she was very indulged.'

'I thought that you hadn't had that much contact with your sister over the years,' Angela remarked. 'How could you know anything about the way they were bringing up Natasha?'

He stopped pacing to shoot her a sudden, sharp look, as though what she had said contained implied criticism. Of course I must be cautious, she thought, but had he *no* experience of criticism? Was he so accustomed to exerting control that any insurgence from the ranks, however minor, was viewed with irritation? As a teacher, she was used to voicing her opinions amongst her fellow teachers, and generally speaking they were accepted and discussed as valid points of view, even if they might be disagreed with.

If Nick Cameron viewed his word as law, then she was uneasily aware that their relationship might have its tense moments.

Still, she dutifully lowered her eyes, before flicking a glance back at him, to find him watching her curiously.

'True,' he murmured, with no hint of impatience in his voice, 'but we did communicate. Believe it or not, the telephone and the postal service are very good ways of keeping in touch when it's physically impossible to be on the scene.'

'Yes, of course.'

This time he looked at her with a sort of frustrated impatience.

'But you don't agree,' he said flatly, and she was tempted to ask whether he cared or not if she agreed with what he had to say. After all, she was only his potential employee, not a prospective sparring partner.

Instead, with a flash of sudden inspiration, she said mildly, 'Of course I agree. Telephones and the postal service are very good ways of keeping in touch. They certainly don't invalidate a relationship.' She half smiled at him. 'How else do you think I kept in touch with your sister?'

She preferred to look at this as an unanswerable question pointing him in the right direction, rather than an out and out lie. She had only ever spoken to Amanda Streetman when she had thought it necessary; when Natasha had been ill with some childhood illness, when an expected letter had failed to arrive. When she'd *had* to know how her daughter was.

He raised one eyebrow, appreciating the point, and then laughed—a low, amused laugh that sent a curious tingle through her body.

'*Touché*, Miss Field.' The grey eyes held hers for a moment. Trying to read her again. 'I can't say that I was a hands-on uncle to Natasha, but I did know that she was cherished. Perhaps even spoiled.'

'Spoiled, Mr Cameron?' Angela looked at him enquiringly, but her fingers tightened on her lap.

'Naturally, when she joined me in New York, she was under immense strain. Her parents had both been killed in unfortunate circumstances and she had suddenly found herself transported across the Atlantic, amongst people she didn't know. But from the start she refused to accept the situation.'

'As you say, a difficult situation for a child to accept.' she tried to keep her voice light but she was more than an interested bystander, even though she could reason and acknowledged that she had relinquished rights of involvement in a single action that she had lived to regret. 'Some children find it very hard to move easily from one scenario to another. Adjustment can take a long time, especially given the circumstances.'

'Are you pointing the finger of blame in my direction, Miss Field?'

'I wouldn't dream of doing that, Mr Cameron. I don't know you. I certainly don't know how hard you tried to smooth trouble waters and help your niece to settle.' Wrong choice of phrase, she immediately thought. She felt a flare of panic and began to perspire lightly. What if he decides that the last person he needs for Natasha is an obstinate schoolteacher with too much forthrightness and too little tact? she asked herself. She felt a wave of nervous dread wash over her.

'Natasha didn't want to settle,' he said bluntly. 'She made that apparent from the start. Hence my decision to return to England. I shall be working very long hours, however, which is why I replied to your letter. I shall need someone to be there for Natasha when I'm not around. I travel extensively, apart from anything else.'

So you really made an effort to help your niece to settle down in a foreign country, Angela thought with angry resentment. She could picture the scene well enough. A lost, lonely child, shunted abroad to an uncle she had probably only ever met a handful of times, and not even a genial, comfortable uncle, but a powerful, workaholic tycoon with sufficient corporate responsibilities to ensure that he was seldom around.

'Of course. I understand.'

He frowned, and then said unexpectedly, 'Has anyone ever told you that you have a curious talent for accusation even when you verbally appear to be co-operating, Miss Field?'

'No,' Angela said without hesitation.

He raked his fingers through his hair and looked as

though he would have liked to have debated the point, but all he did was shrug.

'There is something going on here that I can't quite put my finger on,' he said, staring at her, as though willing her to release her secret. 'I don't care for situations that I don't understand,' he added softly. He moved across to where she was sitting and towered over her, dark, overpowering, with just the merest hint of threat. 'The job is yours, Miss Field. I only hope that you do nothing to persuade me that I have made a mistake.' Or else... his voice promised.

'I hope so too,' Angela said politely. She stood up, and was unprepared for the current that surged through her when he reached out and shook her hand. She felt idiotically as though she had touched a live wire, and had to fight the impulse to yank her hand back and inspect for burn marks.

'When can you start?'

'I need to give the school a month's notice,' Angela said, resting both hands on her bag, which she had slung over one shoulder.

'We haven't touched on the financial arrangements,' he remarked, looking at her narrowly. 'I'm surprised you didn't ask what you would be paid. The terms and conditions of the job.'

Because, she thought, they're irrelevant. My dream is within reach. What does money matter?

'I had no idea I would be offered the job until a few minutes ago,' she said hastily. 'It would have seemed premature to quiz you on any financial arrangements.'

He didn't say anything for a while. He just looked at her with the intensity of an engineer inspecting a piece of equipment and mentally working out how precisely it was run.

'I'll confirm it all in writing,' he said at last. 'You should hear from me by the middle of next week. As I explained in my letter to you, I did feel it best that I…meet you, alone, before introducing you to my niece. When you next come, Natasha will be here.'

'Yes.' Her voice was barely a whisper and she cleared her throat. 'I look forward to that. Very much.'

She had the strangest, wildest feeling that at long last a circle of events, started so long ago, was finally reaching completion. Where the road would lead, she could not predict. But the journey was one already too long in the making.

CHAPTER TWO

SHE had thought that the month would drag past, but in the event the days seemed to fly at the speed of light.

There was so much to be done.

Her notice was accepted with regret. She would, she was told, be sorely missed. Her class, a rowdy mixed group of thirty-odd students, were unnaturally subdued for her last week, and surprised her by buying her a leaving present of some painting equipment. Yes, she thought, I'll miss this. The hum of activity, the energy needed to control a classful of teenagers who mostly thought that they had far more important things to do than work at school.

Stepping forward now was like stepping off a cliff into the unknown, but she hardly had the time to feel regret, or doubt or uncertainty as to whether she was doing the right thing. She seemed to be propelled on some high octane fuel that kept her feet slightly off the ground.

Her biggest headache was her cottage, but in all events that was sorted out far more easily than she had imagined possible.

By a quirk of coincidence, one of the younger teachers who was still living with her parents jumped at the chance of renting it.

'No wild parties or orgies,' Angela warned her, smiling.

Lesley, who gave the impression that she wouldn't recognise a wild party if it descended on her, smiled back. 'When do teachers ever get the chance for wild parties?' she asked.

'And I may want to come back now and again, in which case you'll have to shift over so that we can share the space,' Angela went on. She would, she had discovered from her contract, be allowed four weeks' holiday a year.

The terms and conditions of the job were far better than she would have dreamed possible, and the pay was far more generous than she would have expected. With the rent from Lesley covering the mortgage on the cottage, she would be better off than if she had continued teaching.

It was only when she made the journey to London for the second time, this time with her bags and painting equipment in attendance, that she began to feel nervous.

What if Natasha hated her? Angela felt that she could cope with just about anything, but never with that. And what if Nick Cameron decided that she wasn't up to the job? She was on a trial probation period of three months. He had not struck her as the easiest of people to work for.

Her nerves followed her all through the long train ride to London and through the taxi ride to the house, which was as imposing as she remembered.

'Mr Cameron is expecting you,' the housekeeper said loudly after opening the door. 'If you could make your way to his study, I will deal with your bags.' She then proceeded to instruct the taxi driver to bring the bags round to the side entrance.

'Can I just pay him before I go?' Angela asked.

'Mr Cameron will cover the cost,' the housekeeper said firmly.

'Right, then...' Angela said, hovering nervously, but as she had clearly been dealt with, and Eva was now vanishing with the taxi driver in tow towards the side of the house, she quietly shut the front door and made her way along to the office.

The house was silent. Was Natasha upstairs somewhere? Angela wondered. Doing her homework, perhaps? Maybe she was in the office with her uncle. The last photo she had received had shown a slight, pretty child, with shoulder-length dark hair, surrounded by presents.

Now that she was here, her teaching job, her house, her friends, all seemed a thousand light years away. It was as though this moment in time had suddenly obliterated everything else.

The pine door was ajar, and she knocked and pushed it open to find Nick Cameron standing at the window, glaring outside. When she walked in, he shifted the glare to her.

'Natasha,' he said, by way of polite preliminary, 'should have been home from school. But she decided to go and have tea with one of her schoolfriends, despite my express order not to.' His mouth was a grim line.

'Oh,' Angela said, disappointed. 'And what time do you expect her back?'

He glance at his watch. 'In an hour or so. She'll be dropped back. We might as well go into the sitting room and have some tea there. And wait for her to return.' He shook his head in frustrated anger and stalked out of the office with Angela following behind him.

Did this man ever behave in a normal fashion? she wondered. For starters, was he ever polite? Or did he feel himself to be above such mundane things as good manners and common courtesy?

He made his way to the sitting room, stopping *en route* to tell Eva that she could bring tea for them there.

Angela felt as though she had unwittingly been caught up in a tornado, and by the time they made it to the sitting room she was angry enough to say to him coldly, 'There's really no need for you to feel obliged to entertain me while we wait for Natasha to return. I would be just as happy sitting here on my own. Or perhaps Eva could show me to my room and I could begin unpacking my things.'

He turned to face her, and again she felt that confusing awareness of his masculinity which she had conveniently succeeded in forgetting over the past few weeks.

'Either of which option would be preferable to being cooped up in this room with me for company?' His anger seemed to have dissipated and he looked at her levelly, with a hint of amusement.

'Please don't misinterpret my words, Mr Cameron...'

'Nick. We might as well dispense with the formalities since we'll be living under the same roof.' He sat down on the sofa and indicated for her to do the same.

Angela went across to one of the chairs and sat down, crossing her legs. She was wearing a pale green dress, belted at the waist, and had brushed her hair into a neat French plait. She knew that she looked younger than her age, a teenager almost, and she had to remind herself that she was a schoolteacher and fully capable of dealing with most situations. She told herself that she was certainly more than capable of dealing with an impolite man with no regard for other people.

'Actually,' he drawled, 'this is as good an opportunity as any for us to have an informal chat, don't you agree? There were one or two things that I didn't mention when we last met.'

'Yes?' Angela said warily.

'First of all, the fact that I shan't be around very much. I'm often abroad and out most nights of the week. Eva does no cooking for me unless specifically requested, but she'll prepare your dinner and Natasha's before she leaves at five.'

'I'm quite capable of preparing my own food, Mr Cameron...Nick. I've been doing it a number of years, believe it or not.'

'Secondly, Mandy and Clive never believed in laying down laws about bedtime, and I've felt obliged to allow that to continue rather than introduce yet another disruption into Natasha's life. However, now that you're taking charge, I'm sure that you have other thoughts on the matter.'

'In other words,' Angela said drily, 'I'm to feel free to make myself immediately unpopular by forcing Natasha into bed by eight every night.'

He shot her a half-smile of amused charm.

'As a matter of fact,' she continued, feeling vaguely unbalanced by that smile, 'I do think that children of her age need discipline in their lives, or else there is a tendency to stretch tolerance to the limits. Eight o'clock on weekdays seems fair to me, perhaps a bit later on weekends. Would you agree?'

'I leave it in your capable hands,' he said with a shrug. 'As I've said, I'm not around with any amount of regularity. I shall have to trust you in my absence.'

'What were the arrangements before I arrived?' Angela asked curiously.

'I paid Eva extra to stay on and I tried to be back here by eight most nights.'

'How awkward for you,' she heard herself say with exaggerated horror.

'Do I sense another backhanded insult coming my way, Miss Field...Angela?'

'No, of course not,' she stammered uncomfortably. 'I merely meant that it must have been difficult for you...'

Eva bustled in with the tray, and while she poured tea Nick looked at Angela with a depth of concentration that made her want to fidget.

As soon as the housekeeper had left the room, shutting the door behind her, he leaned forward with his elbows resting on his thighs and said in a hard voice, 'I'm unmarried, with no experience of children and with an excessively demanding job. To find myself in the unexpected role of guardian to an eight-year-old child has not been an easy transition. I realise that as a teacher you no doubt have intransigent views on how to bring up children, but I certainly will not tolerate glib judgements made about the job I've done of it.'

'I hadn't realised that I was making glib judgements,' Angela said coolly. 'I understand that it must have been very difficult for you, altering your lifestyle to accommodate a child...'

'Which is why I've employed you. So that you can fill any gaps I leave behind.'

'I see.' She sipped her tea and looked at him over the rim of her cup. 'However, you *are* her uncle and I would expect you to have some involvement in her upbringing. I do not expect you to vanish off the face of the earth the minute you think you can conveniently do so.'

It had had to be said and she had anticipated a furious response to it, but all he did was lean back in the sofa and look at her with a glimmer of a grin.

'My God, woman,' he said lazily, 'you certainly know how to crack the whip. I feel as though I ought to jump to attention!'

Angela felt herself redden. A bore, she thought. He imagines me to be a prim bore, the sort of woman he probably steers clear of.

'There's no need to be sarcastic,' she said defensively, tilting her chin up. 'I shall just try and do what's best for your niece, and all I'm saying is that I shall need your co-operation.'

He was still grinning. 'And you look so young and guileless. It just shows, doesn't it, that appearances can be deceptive?'

Angela looked away briefly. He had no idea how close to the truth he had skimmed just then, and she wasn't about to enlighten him.

'I can't help the way I look,' she said steadily. 'I simply believe in speaking my mind. That way there's less room for misunderstanding.'

'And have you always been like that?' he asked, his grey eyes speculative. 'Or did your job breed that particular trait?'

'I've never stopped to ask myself the question,' she said vaguely. She didn't want this conversation to stray too far from the topic in hand; she didn't want him to think that he could start prying into her personal life. Best to keep it all under wraps or else she might find herself skating on thin ice—and that could prove to be a very dangerous pastime indeed.

'Go ahead and ask it now.'

'I really don't think that my personal life is any of your business,' she said levelly.

'And I think that it is,' he replied, with equal calm and a great deal of sharp insistence. 'I'm going to entrust my niece to you. I'd quite like to know what sort of woman I'm putting my trust in. You knew my sister, but that's not really enough, is it?'

'You could always write to the school for references,' Angela said reasonably. 'Or else phone them. I could give you the number.'

'Did you have a happy childhood?' He continued looking at her carefully.

'It had its moments,' she muttered uncomfortably.

'By which you mean that it's a hands-off topic?' His eyes glinted and he clasped his hands behind his head. The master of the house.

It was strange how well he complemented the richly furnished room with its deep Egyptian colours and dark furniture. He seemed to bring it to life, but then she imagined he would dominate any room he happened to be in. There was no way that he would ever take second place to the furnishings. His personality was too powerful for that. It overrode everything and everyone.

'Is that why you went into teaching?' he asked, and when she didn't reply went on, 'Because you wanted the chance to improve the quality of children's lives, when your own childhood had been so lacking?'

'I never said that!' she flared.

'You're free to deny it.'

She maintained a silence that only just bordered on polite. If the circumstances had been different she would have walked out of the room and kept on walking until she had put enough distance between herself and this man to make her forget him.

'What about men?' he asked. 'Do you have a boyfriend? Was he happy about your upping roots and moving to London virtually on a whim?'

'It wasn't a whim!' she denied hotly.

'No? Then what,' he asked in a soft voice, '*was* it?'

'I meant that I gave it a great deal of thought before I

wrote to you. And, although this is none of your business, I don't happen to have a boyfriend.'

'Fine. That brings me neatly to another point. No men traipsing in and out of this house.'

'I am not the kind of woman who has men traipsing in and out of *any* house,' Angela told him coldly.

'Never?'

Angela's lips compressed and she looked at him in resolute silence.

The subject of men was one she steered well away from. When her single friends were recounting their escapades with whoever, doing whatever, wherever, she had nothing to contribute. Her one sexual relationship with a man, all those years ago, had been a catastrophe which she had later discovered had spawned problems long after the affair had ended.

She could barely bring herself to think about it without wincing. Simon Grey—charming, practised Simon Grey—who had won her over, wooed her with the kind of romance she had never had in her life before, taken her to places which were like a different world, wined and dined her and then, when she had pulled back from sleeping with him, had forced her, pinning her down. Payment due on expectations she had engendered. Her own fault, he had explained as she had lain there, feeling dirty and ashamed. She should never have led him on. Admittedly things had got out of control, he had said, but she was a big girl, should have known the rules of the game.

It was so unfair that the legacy he had left her should have been so disastrous.

Her baby given up for adoption and an inability to relate to any man apart from on a purely platonic level. The minute things started getting physical, something inside her reared up and she shied away like a frightened horse.

Nick was watching her intently. 'So what do you do when you're not teaching?' he asked, and Angela gave a little shrug.

'Go out with my friends, read books at home. I try and get to the theatre as often as I can.' On a résumé, she thought, she would hardly sound like a bundle of laughs.

'Right,' he said briskly. Had he tired of the probing now that he had unearthed a supremely boring individual? she wondered. 'Now, about collecting Natasha from school. Eva has been using my chauffeur since we've been in this country, but it would help if you could drive. Do you? You mentioned that you had no car.'

'Yes, I do,' Angela said, breathing a sigh of relief and feeling like a mouse that had suddenly discovered a way out of the trap. 'I did have a car, up until a year or so ago, but it died on me and I've been having lifts with my friend who lives just around the corner.'

'Good. In that case, we shall have to get you something so that you can drive to and from her school.'

'Really?' she asked faintly. 'Isn't that a bit extravagant?'

'Something small shouldn't cost an arm and a leg,' he pointed out, and it took her a few seconds to realise that what would be an extravagance for her would mean nothing at all to him. Such was the difference between them.

'There's no need to look so shocked,' he said mildly. 'I don't intend to hand you over the keys to a Rolls Royce.'

'No, of course not. It's just that...' Her voice trailed off, and when he didn't volunteer to fill the silence she continued a little sheepishly, 'Well, for me at any rate, a car represents something that needs saving for. I could never dream of just going out and buying one, even the smallest, cheapest model, like I would go and buy a new tub of washing powder.' She laughed, embarrassed.

'I'm not saying that I sit around and count my pennies every night, but a teacher's salary doesn't allow for huge extravagances. I can't imagine what it must be like to...well...' She laughed again, and blushed slightly, and was saved from having to resume her strict countenance by the sound of footsteps and voices outside the room. Then the door was pushed open and an eight-year-old child flew in, followed by Eva who wore a look of desperation.

Angela half rose to her feet, then subsided once more onto the chair, because she didn't trust her legs to do what they had to do and keep her standing.

My Natasha, she thought. She didn't even want to blink in case it all faded away and she woke to find that she had been dreaming the whole thing. She hardly dared to breathe.

Of course she would have recognised her daughter from all the photographs she had been sent over the years—the dark hair, longer now than in the most recent photo which was months old, cut in a shoulder-length bob, the dark eyes, the thin frame. But seeing her in the flesh was like being struck by a bolt from the sky. There were so many things that a photo could never capture. The vitality, the mobility of expression, of movement, a feeling of reality.

She doesn't look at all like me, Angela thought, but then again she didn't look a great deal like her father either, apart from the colour of her hair and eyes. She was unique.

'Where have you been, young lady?' Nick asked

coldly. 'I thought I had made it quite clear that I wanted you home directly after school.'

Angela pressed herself back into her chair and tried to fade into the background. She just wanted to observe.

'I promised Emma that I would have tea at her house.' The voice was soft and stubborn. The expression was sulky, of someone prepared to argue. She hadn't glanced in Angela's direction. All her attention was focused on Nick, and Angela had the impression that this atmosphere of combat was not new to either of them. She had to resist the impulse to say that it was all right, that *she* didn't mind what time Natasha returned home—just as she had to resist the impulse to run across the room and hug her and cry.

'That's not the point,' Nick began, keeping his anger in check and employing a voice that was patient if a little weary.

'*You* can't tell me what to do.'

'You live under my roof, and just so long as you do, you'll fall in with my discipline!'

'I have homework to do,' Natasha said, ignoring what he had said.

'I'm glad you mentioned that,' Nick said in the same controlled voice. 'I had a call from your teacher. Again. It appears that you're making no effort in class, your work is sloppy when you put yourself out to do it at all, you—'

'Who cares?'

Nick's mouth tightened.

'You should,' Angela said quietly, and both sets of eyes swung in her direction.

'Who are you?' Natasha asked with hostile suspicion.

'This is Angela Field. Does the name ring a bell?' Nick asked. 'She's the woman you were supposed to return here to meet this afternoon after school. You two should have been getting to know one another, instead of which you disobeyed my express orders and—'

'You can't order me around!' Natasha shouted, reverting her attention to Nick. 'And I don't have to *get to know* anybody if I don't want to!'

'You'll have to excuse my niece,' Nick said grimly to Angela.

'I understand.' Angela looked sympathetically at Natasha and sat on her hands so that she didn't obey her reflexes and reach out to the child.

'I don't need a nanny,' Natasha burst out sullenly.

'Yes, you do. I can't be around all of the time. You know that…'

'What's wrong with Eva?'

'Eva has put her own life on hold for the past few months so that she could be here for you.'

'So I'm a burden to everybody!' Natasha exploded, but there were tears in her voice. 'I wish I'd never had to live with you! I wish…!' The childish voice faltered and she rushed out of the room. Angela stood up in distress to follow her, but Nick waved her back and she reluctantly sat down again, staring at the door which had been slammed shut.

'I think it would be a good idea if one of us went to her,' Angela said, clearing her throat. 'She needs to be comforted.'

'I have spent the better part of a year excusing Natasha's behaviour,' Nick said tightly. 'It's about time that she learnt a little discipline and a little compromise.'

'She's upset and confused.'

'The longer she's allowed to get away with these tantrums, the more impossible she's going to become. And believe me when I tell you that this is mild compared with her normal behaviour.'

'She's a child!' Angela protested heavily. 'She doesn't see the world in the same way as an adult, and she can't rationalise her feelings the same way that you or I could!'

'And how long do you propose she be allowed to run riot?' he asked unsmilingly. 'For a few more months? A few more years? Until she becomes an utterly unbearable, uncontrollable teenager whose wayward lack of discipline could land her in some serious trouble?'

He stood up and walked across to an ornately carved cupboard which turned out to be a drinks cabinet. He poured himself a whisky and soda and offered her something, which she refused with a shake of her head.

He swallowed the contents of his glass in a couple of mouthfuls, then poured himself another which he took with him back to the sofa.

'I don't think I ever drank as much as I do now before Natasha came along,' he said with a trace of dry irony in his voice. He twirled the glass in his hand and stared broodingly at the golden liquid, as though optimistic that if he looked hard enough he would find the answer to a riddle that had been bothering him.

Angela looked at him with an anguished feeling of being torn in two. On the one hand she felt an instinctive empathy with Natasha, her daughter, her flesh and blood, however much the years stood between them, and on the other a reluctant admission that in some ways he was right, even if he was setting about proving his point in entirely the wrong way.

'Do you love her?' she asked curiously, and he raised his eyes to look at her.

'What kind of a question is that? Something that you

picked up at your teacher training college to deal with situations like this?'

'There's no need for you to be sarcastic,' she said in a low voice, pushing the boat out and hoping that his simmering anger against his niece wouldn't manifest itself as anger against her. 'I'm just trying to see both sides of a story.'

'I am responsible for her,' Nick said, draining the glass and then depositing it heavily on the table next to the sofa. He sat back, folded his arms and stared at her with a mocking glitter in his eyes. 'I don't suppose that's quite the right answer, but it's the truthful one. Until the accident, I had precious little contact with my niece. I sent presents over at Christmas and on birthdays, and I saw her occasionally, but never on a one-to-one basis and never for any meaningful length of time. I was fond of her, but she was far removed from me.'

'And so you must be able to understand how she feels now,' Angela said, blinking back an inclination to cry and controlling her voice. 'Children can sense things, even though they may not always be able to articulate their feelings. Natasha senses a lack of love. Is it any wonder that she sees herself as a burden?'

'So that's your remedy, is it?' he asked, with a crooked smile that conveyed little warmth and no humour. 'Love to order?'

'A bit of effort in the right direction might be a start!' she snapped, standing up.

'Where do you think you're going?'

'I'm going to see her,' Angela said, gathering some of her composure and making an effort to remind herself that she couldn't be seen to be acting in too partisan a manner or else he would begin to pick up signals, which he would then pursue like a dog chasing a bone.

'Sit back down!'

She hesitated, lowering her eyes to conceal the mutiny in them. He was unbearable! She was trying very hard to see his point of view. She was trying very hard to recognise that *his* life had been altered as well and that the changes were not easy for him to deal with. But at the end of the day he was still unbearable.

'Sit back down,' he said more calmly. 'Please.' The word sounded foreign to him but she sat down reluctantly. 'We need to talk about how you're going to deal with the situation.'

'How *we're* going to deal with the situation,' she amended, and he shrugged. 'Look,' she continued on a sigh, 'of course I agree that Natasha must learn some discipline. From the little I've seen—and you tell me that this has been her normal behaviour...'

'It has.'

'Well, you're right in that, if she's left to her own devices, her wilfulness can quite simply gather momentum until it's virtually unstoppable...'

'So we agree on something. I'm glad to hear it!'

Angela frowned at him coldly. 'But any discipline has got to be administered in the right way. There's no point in laying down a series of laws and then flying off the handle if she breaks one of them, without taking the trouble to understand why.'

'This is like being back at school,' Nick muttered under his breath, and he shot her a dark look from under his lashes.

'Does *no one* stand up to you?' she asked in amazement.

'Naturally, people feel free to express opinions.'

Say no more, she thought drily. Expressing an opinion was quite different from flagrantly contradicting. She imagined that he could very easily inspire the sort of awe in people that left them shying away from too much vigorous argument. He was ruthless, powerful, with a mind that could win any debate without exerting itself too much. Perhaps, under different circumstances, she too might have cowered, but Natasha was her daughter and she would act in the way she saw best, even if that meant delivering a few unpleasant home truths to him along the way.

She stood up, and this time, thankfully, he did as well, following her to the door. But when she was there, ready to leave, he reached down and held the doorknob in his fingers.

'And does anyone tell *you* what to do?' he asked softly, looking down at her.

She raised her eyes and her breath caught in her throat. She found that she couldn't utter a word.

'What's underneath that sensible head on young shoulders?' he enquired curiously. 'Tell me. I should love to know.'

'I'm—I'm a teacher...' Angela stammered falteringly.

'And what does the teacher become when she walks out of the classroom and leaves the blackboard behind?'

'I...'

He leaned against the door and regarded her closely, until her cheeks were burning.

'I...I...what?' he asked.

'I think I should go,' she said in a firm voice, without looking at him.

He laughed and stood back with a little bow.

'Perhaps you should,' he murmured. 'And I'll let you escape.' He paused and then said with amusement, 'For now.'

CHAPTER THREE

THINGS had not got off to a swimming start, Angela thought the following day.

What had she expected? She didn't know. But it had been hard in a way that she had not imagined. Hard in that she felt drawn to Natasha by powerful maternal strings which she discovered she had never let go, and it hurt in ways that she couldn't have foreseen that Natasha treated her with the supreme indifference that only children could master with such ease.

Last night had been a write-off. Natasha had retired to her bedroom and there she had stayed for the remainder of the evening until it was time to go to sleep.

And hadn't that been another fiasco?

Angela had gone up to the bedroom, pointedly at eight o'clock, to say goodnight, and had been frostily told that there were no rules about bedtimes.

'There are now,' she had said, standing by the door and wishing that Natasha would at least look at her instead of reading her book.

'Says who?'

'Says me.'

'I'm not tired.'

'You will be,' Angela had said, walking into the bedroom and positioning herself directly in front of Natasha. 'Tomorrow. At school. When you should be concentrating on work.'

So lights had duly been switched off but the battle had not been won. She had left the bedroom amidst a strained atmosphere of sulky antagonism which had carried over to the morning.

I've seen pictures of my daughter, she thought sadly, snippets of a baby growing into childhood, but I've never known her. Had all the laughter faded when Clive and Amanda had died? It would be a long process getting it back.

She walked across to the sitting room window and stared outside. It was a pretty scene, with the sun dappling the lawn and an illusory atmosphere of peace and quiet.

Eva was busy in some other part of the house, cleaning, and in a moment Nick would be arriving so that they could go out and choose a car to buy.

'Are you sure about the car?' Angela had asked him nervously the night before, and he had made some wry remark about school drops being rather difficult without one.

'I have no objection to taking Natasha in on the underground,' she had replied, even though she had taken the underground only a few times in her entire life and had found it a grubby, unrewarding experience.

'Tomorrow,' was all he had said. 'Ten-thirty. I'll pick you up here.'

She looked at her watch, then at the door, and, as though the co-ordinated concentration had worked, she heard the sound of a car drawing up outside the house. Her stomach went into a series of knots.

Nick Cameron made her nervous. However hard she summoned up that crisp, schoolteacher approach, she still couldn't look at him without responding on some strange, gut level that made her feel a little disorientated.

It wasn't Nick, however, who was waiting for her in the hall when she went out. It was George, his chauffeur, who informed her that he would have to drive her to the office because one of Nick's meetings had overrun and he hadn't been able to get out to the house himself.

'It happens more often than not,' George explained, once they were in the car.

No wonder, she thought idly, he wanted a nanny for Natasha. It must have been awkward for Eva if she had had to hang around in the evenings, waiting for overrun meetings to wind up. Poor Natasha. To go from one home where she was cosseted and adored to another where she was an inconvenience. Was it any wonder that she was so defensive and antagonistic?

The office, when they arrived, turned out to be three floors in a very large, heavily glass-fronted building. Nick's office was, as she might have expected, on the top floor, along with those of the other directors working for him. The secretaries all worked in a pool of sorts, and the personal assistants had slightly more elevated positions outside the main offices of the directors for whom they worked.

Angela walked past them and thought how different the atmosphere was from that of the general, slightly chaotic staffroom at the school. These, she realised, were the silent, well-oiled wheels of big business. Behind closed doors, the very rich and the very powerful were doing deals that were probably worth thousands, if not millions. It was hard not to feel awe-inspired.

By the time she came to the very last office, and notably the largest, she felt as though she had had a sudden and revealing lesson in how high commerce worked. Everything hushed, efficient, insulated. There were no clocks to be seen anywhere. Here, time was unimportant.

If there was work to be done, then it was done, and not according to a timescale.

The personal assistant who was sitting at her desk outside looked up when Angela tentatively made her way forward and stood up, perfectly groomed and poised, hand outstretched. She must have been in her mid-forties, and everything about her was impeccable—from the dove-grey suit and matching shoes to the neatly lacquered hair and perfectly made-up face.

'Miss Field,' she said with a smile, walking around her desk to shake Angela's hand. 'Mr Cameron is expecting you. I won't offer you tea or coffee. I believe he wishes to leave immediately.'

Angela briefly shook the hand and was ushered into Nick's office to find him on the telephone, his dark head bent over a stack of papers on his desk. The door clicked shut behind her and he looked up, caught her eye and waved her to sit down in the chair opposite him. Then he carried on talking into the telephone, and she allowed her eyes to drift around the office.

It was large, with one entire wall given over to a huge pane of glass, overlooking, she imagined, an inspiring if monotonous view of the city. There were a couple of paintings, but bland, impersonal affairs, and shelves of books relating mostly to company laws, taxes, buy-outs and various other things which meant nothing at all to her.

It could have been anyone's office. There were no personal touches to be seen anywhere, but then she didn't think that he was the sort of man who believed in displaying his private life for the public to see, even if that only meant the odd photograph of someone close to him. While she was giving the room her once-over he fin-

ished his telephone call, and she looked at him to find
that he was watching her with a trace of amusement.

'Well?' he asked. 'Does it pass muster?'

'What?' Angela replied, thrown into sudden confusion
as much by the fact that she had surprised him looking
at her as at the question.

'The office. From the expression on your face, you
didn't seem to be overly impressed.' He laughed as she
reddened, and stood up, but instead of heading towards
the door he moved to the huge windows and beckoned
her across to stand next to him.

A single crook of the finger, she thought irritably. I
call and the world does my bidding.

She went to stand next to him, making sure that she
didn't get too close, and obediently stared down at precisely the sort of view she had expected. A sprawling
panorama of busy city life.

'I chose this building, and this office,' he explained,
'because of this view. London at its most vibrant. Don't
you agree?' He half turned to look down at her while she
continued staring out of the window and searching for
something to say. She personally found the view of
streets and buildings and cars and hurrying people rather
depressing.

'It's certainly very busy,' she volunteered in a polite
voice. 'It must be easy to be lonely in a city as busy as
this.' She had no idea what had made her impart this
particular piece of uncalled for wisdom, and she hurriedly
stepped back and resumed, in a brisker voice, 'I'm very
sorry to have interrupted your day like this. You should
have called to cancel.'

'Loneliness is a frame of mind that can breed anywhere,' he said, turning to face her. 'I hope you'll feel

free to tell me if you start missing your friends and family. I'm sure that something can be arranged.'

'Of course,' Angela mumbled.

'It's presumably quite a change for you. Not only have you moved jobs, from one extreme to the other, but you've also moved location as well.' He strolled across the room and slipped his jacket on. It was funny, but, even with his back turned, she still had that uncanny feeling that he could see into her mind and probe her thoughts.

'Well, London isn't exactly a million miles away from the Midlands,' Angela said with a nervous little laugh. She was standing now too, hovering. Wondering why she still couldn't quite relax, even though he was actually being kind to her, showing a consideration for her feelings that she hadn't counted on.

'True.' He shrugged and his grey eyes swept over her, then returned to her face. 'But I dare say your bonds there are very strong if you've lived there all your life. Have you lived there all your life?'

'Yes, I have,' she admitted cautiously, sensing the treacherous proximity of quicksand.

'Of course, you have one weekend in four when you'll be completely free to do whatever you want—return to your home, visit your friends and family.'

Angela didn't say anything. She hadn't considered doing anything on that one weekend in four. She couldn't bear the thought of letting Natasha out of her sight again. Not now—not now that she had found her, albeit in circumstances which she could never have envisaged even in her most daring flights of imagination, and of those there had been quite a few over the years.

'Do you know anyone at all in London?' he asked idly, his hands in the pockets of his jacket. He had moved a little closer to her. When she breathed deeply, she could smell that clean, masculine scent of him which was as potent as incense.

'No. No, I don't.' She gave a self-conscious laugh and looked down at her feet, clad in a pair of low brown sandals. Her hair, which she hadn't bothered to tie back, swung across her face and she automatically tucked it behind her ears.

'Your family all live in the Midlands?' he asked, without any particular curiosity in his voice.

'I'm afraid I have no family,' Angela said lightly, thinking of her daughter, cherishing the thought the way a child cherished some delightful secret.

'I'm sorry.'

'Why?' She raised her eyes to his. 'I mean...thank you...yes. Should we...be on our way...? I know you have to fit a lot into your day... Perhaps we should...?' She was rambling, her words tumbling into each other. Rather than be reduced to complete incoherence she lapsed into silence, and, to her relief, he nodded and glanced at his watch.

'I'll just leave a few letters with Pauline,' he said, moving towards the door and opening it for her to brush past him.

She watched as he left instructions with his assistant, bending over her desk, running through a stack of letters with her. Pauline didn't look at him at all. She nodded, efficiently asked questions and checked her desk diary so that she could fill him in on clients who needed contacting, but Angela noticed, wryly that her face was a little flushed by the time Nick straightened up from the desk.

So, she thought, the ferocious impact of his personality was not lost even on his personal assistant, who was no doubt happily married with a string of children, if not a

few grandchildren somewhere in the background. Men
like that should have health warnings tattooed on their
foreheads. Men with looks and charm and the ability to
use both to their advantage.

If Simon Grey had had a health warning on his forehead... If only she could have been warned against him
instead of blithely rushing in, naïvely in love with the
feeling of being in love... If only. She closed her eyes,
feeling dizzy, and when she opened them it was to find
Nick looking at her and standing considerably closer to
her than she had anticipated.

'Are you all right?' he asked sharply, and she nodded
with a smile.

'Oh, yes. I'm fine.'

'You don't look fine. You've gone as white as a sheet.'
He reached out and put his hand on her arm as though
she needed steadying, which she hadn't until that point.
Now his fingers burnt through the thin cotton of her
sleeves and she really did feel a bit shaky on her legs,
which annoyed her immensely.

She pulled away and repeated in a slightly irritable
voice, 'Really, I'm fine. Just a passing headache.'

'In that case, let's go,' he said shortly, turning away,
and she foolishly felt a pang of misery at the thought that
she might have offended him. Pah! she thought. *Offended*
him? Jarred his male pride, if anything. He probably
wasn't used to women pulling away from his slightest
touch as though he was the carrier of some highly con-
tagious and rather unpleasant disease.

He certainly seemed polite enough as they stood by
the lift, waiting for it to arrive. He chatted to her about
cars, to which she made virtually no response since she
knew precious little about them apart from their being
either reliable or unreliable ways of getting from A to B.

If she hadn't been looking at him quite so intently she almost certainly wouldn't have registered the flicker of change in his expression just as the lift doors pinged open. It was too momentary to be deciphered, too fleeting a glimpse of some emotion registered in passing then concealed once again as his eyes shifted away from her to a point over her left shoulder. She turned instinctively to see what had caught his attention.

She certainly hadn't heard approaching footsteps, but then the carpet was thick, luxurious, and the woman she saw standing in front of her immediately struck her as the sort who glided rather than clumped. She was also the sort of woman who made other women feel instantly at their worst.

'Philippa.' Nick smiled, creating, Angela thought, a bubble around the striking woman and himself, so that she felt automatically thrust onto the fringes.

'Nick, I wanted to catch you before you left.' Philippa had glanced briefly in Angela's direction and then dismissed her. 'About this meeting tomorrow—shall I bring my forecasts for the next quarter or would you rather we go through them together in private first?'

American, Angela thought in surprise, despite the very English name.

'Bring them to the meeting,' he said, then at last he turned to Angela and murmured a few introductions, which had the adverse effect of making her feel even more of a third party.

'We're on our way to buy a car,' he said. 'You'll have to fill me in on that Drew business later.'

'Yes, of course.' Philippa turned to Angela and bestowed upon her her first look of open inspection. 'So you're the woman who wrote to Nick about a job looking after Natasha. Good luck. I can't say it's a job I'd give my body and soul to have, but then again I can't think of anything more dreary than caretaking a child.'

Angela could find no response to this that wouldn't emerge sounding rude, so she maintained her frozen smile and glazed expression and murmured something non-committal and fairly inaudible.

The voice was friendly enough, and there was a smile on the face, but Philippa's expression was still one of cold, calculating appraisal. She had a peculiar beauty that did not lend itself easily to warmth. She was just a little too perfect and more than just a little too aware of the fact.

She was tall, slim, with very straight black hair cut in a very short bob and large, green, feline eyes. Her face was alabaster-smooth. It was nearly impossible to guess her age. Anywhere between late twenties and mid-thirties.

'Still, I expect you're used to children. I gather you were a schoolteacher before?'

'That's right,' Angela said, maintaining her rigidly polite expression with difficulty.

When Nick interrupted to say that they had to leave, she breathed a sigh of relief.

'I'll see you later, then?' Philippa asked, reverting her attention to Nick, her body language telling all as she reached to touch him lightly on his arm. 'To discuss the budgets and Drew Computers?'

'If I'm back,' he said, frowning.

'How about dinner, in that case?'

There was a fraction of hesitation, then he said, 'Fine.'

'My place?'

'No. Luigi's. Get Pauline to book a table for eight. Now, Philippa, we really have to go. I'll meet you at the restaurant.'

It shocked Angela to realise how curious she was about the other woman. Not with an idle curiosity, but a burning need to find out more. What, for instance, was her relationship with Nick? Were they lovers? Nick Cameron was a rich, eligible bachelor. Phillipa worked for him, but she was American, which implied that she had made the transatlantic move to be with him. She was also beautiful.

Angela could only speculate, but she reasoned that amongst circles such as theirs two eligible, good-looking people would have no mental qualms about having an affair. Wasn't that the way it worked in the urbane, sophisticated world that they inhabited? A mutual spark followed by satisfying sex and a relationship in which the word love was never mentioned?

Or maybe, she mused, frowning angrily at this train of thought which seemed to have her in its grip and wouldn't let her go, love and marriage were on the agenda as well. Nick would hardly flaunt his emotions in public. He was too guarded for that, but they *were* meeting for dinner to discuss work—so-called. Was that wholly in line with company policy?

The questions which she hadn't invited and didn't want to ask herself filled her head, until she had to make a supreme effort to concentrate. She made brief stabs at small talk in the back of his chauffeur-driven car, then threw all her attention into the task of understanding the merits of various cars as soon as they were at the showroom: engine size, fuel consumption, availability of spare parts. Nick talked knowledgeably on the subject—so knowledgeably, in fact, that at one point the salesman asked him whether he was in the car business himself, a question he managed to avoid answering.

A little under an hour later, she found herself in possession of a brand new hatchback, bright red, to be delivered that evening. The first new car she had ever owned in her life and doubtless the last. A purchase which would have taken her months to contemplate and just as long to justify had been accomplished in the time it would have taken for her to teach an art class at school.

He must have noticed the dazed expression on her face, because as soon as they were outside he turned to her and said drily, 'Care for a spot of lunch? You look as though you could use it.'

'Thank you,' Angela said, still bemused at the speed with which things could be done provided the money was there. 'That would be very nice.'

'Now,' he said, when they were sitting inside a wine bar close to his office, 'all you need to do is learn to manoeuvre around the London road system.'

She looked at him, less nervously than usual, and laughed.

'I shall drive very slowly from house to school and back and make sure that I don't deviate.'

'That should make for a happy queue of traffic behind you,' he said, calling the waiter across and ordering drinks.

'I'm not aggressive enough to tackle the roads here. I marvel at how George does it. Did you find him over here or did you bring him back from America as well?'

'As well?'

'As well as Philippa,' she said awkwardly. 'I assumed that she had relocated with you when I heard her accent.'

'Yes, she did.' He sat back in his chair and looked at her. 'There was no need. One of my companies over there would have absorbed her. She's a very talented financial controller. She chose to make the move, though, and she's been a tremendous asset to the company.'

'Yes, I'm sure.' Angela fiddled with the stem of her wine glass, not exactly looking at him, but glancing across every so often. His face, as always, was unrevealing. What had he meant that there had been no need for her to relocate? That they weren't involved on a personal level? Or that, even if they were, she was disposable?

That, she considered, was more likely. Sex was a disposable commodity, easily replaced. Once, she had been misguided enough to think that physical attraction and love went hand in hand. Over the years she had come to realise that nothing could be further form the truth.

'Oh, you are, are you,' Nick commented lazily. 'And this based on a brief meeting of under five minutes.'

'Must be the schoolteacher in me,' Angela said with a small smile. 'At the beginning of each new term, we're the sort who generally cast our eye over the fresh intake and make a few snap judgements on personalities.'

'And you're never wrong.'

'Occasionally. Often I'm right about the difficult ones, but then again, a bit of time and energy can work wonders when it comes to integrating them into the class.'

'Which is the line you intend to take with my niece?'

Angela waited until their orders for food had been taken, thinking about his question, schooling her expression into revealing nothing but the professionalism of someone paid to do a job.

'More or less,' she answered, folding her hands on the table and linking her fingers together. 'Natasha's circumstances are more exceptional than most, wouldn't you agree? She needs very careful, very gentle handling.' She paused and then said, not risking a direct look at his face, 'Was she a happy child before…before the accident?'

Nick's eyes narrowed. 'Isn't that something you should

know? Considering you were in close touch with Amanda?'

She felt a quick chill down her spine. It had been a dangerous question, but one that needed an answer. She should have known that he would not simply reply, not without first considering why the question had been asked in the first place.

'Friends say so much to each other,' she said quickly, 'but often they'll only reveal personal problems to members of their family.'

'My sister, it appears, was quite open with you when it came to certain personal problems. Why wouldn't she have told you if she was having difficulties with Natasha?'

Angela didn't say anything.

'Well?' he persisted.

'Perhaps she didn't like to mention problems, considering that Natasha was adopted. It may have been a sensitive subject with her.'

He let that one go, but she could tell that his antennae had been twitching. Again. She would have to watch her step more carefully in the future. It was a shame because she really would have liked to ask him whether his sister had ever mentioned Natasha expressing curiosity about her natural mother, about *her*, but that would have roused even more suspicion at this point, so she was forced to let the matter drop.

Instead, she made an effort to chat casually about normal, run of the mill topics. She asked him about New York and was amused by his descriptions which, she noticed, contained almost no personal details.

It was only when they were having a cup of coffee at the end of the meal that he said, out of the blue, 'I can't seem to figure you out at all. You're in your mid-twenties, at an age when most women are out enjoying themselves if they don't happen to have found themselves married with two point four children, and yet you seem to have lived a strangely solitary life. And obviously one where your own personal commitments were so non-existent that you felt free to abandon everything on what must surely have been a whim, despite your denials to the contrary.'

'There are lots of women my age who aren't married and who haven't got an engagement ring on their finger,' Angela told him coolly. 'This may come as a shock to you, but not all women see their role in life as finding a partner for marriage.'

'But quite a few of them do, whether they care to admit it or not.'

'Maybe,' she said, 'but not me.'

'Why not?'

'Why are you so concerned with things that have no bearing on my being here?'

'Everything in the past has a bearing on the present,' Nick said, staring at her, and, although his voice was casual, his eyes were intent. 'How do I know that you're not running away from a soured relationship with a man? In which case, how do I know that there won't be a grand reconciliation which will leave Natasha stranded?'

'You'll just have to trust that I'm telling you the truth,' Angela muttered. Why couldn't he have let their conversation remain impersonal and unthreatening? Why did he have to be so damned persistent? 'Anyway, why are you so curious? You can't be *this* curious about all your employees? Surely?'

'Not all my employees come to me under such odd circumstances.'

Angela hoped that she wasn't expected to rustle up an

answer to that one, because for the life of her she couldn't think of anything to say by way of response, so she drained the remainder of her coffee, offered him the sweetest of smiles, and thanked him for a delicious meal.

'I hope it hasn't spoilt your appetite for your dinner tonight,' she said politely, which met with the dark frown of someone who, temporarily, had to concede defeat.

He paid the bill, and outside George was waiting for them. A luxury, Angela thought, that it would be easy to get accustomed to. No running to catch a bus, or fighting the crowds on the underground, or even having to scout around for a taxi. Just a chauffeur, obligingly waiting to take you in air-conditioned comfort to wherever your destination might be.

They stepped into the car, and she turned to him and said, without thinking, 'Have you always had a chauffeur at your disposal?'

'Not *always*, no. But for the past few years, I have. Makes getting around a hell of a lot easier. It also means that I can work in the car.'

Angela nodded and said, half inclining away from him to look out of the window and feeling guiltily superior, 'I can imagine. If someone had told me that I'd ever find myself in the back of a chauffeur-driven car, I would have fainted on the spot.'

'And now that you have, how does it feel?'

She turned to look at him and was a little taken aback to find that he wasn't smiling good-humouredly at this train of conversation. Perhaps he had used up his quota of smiles, she thought. At least as far as she was concerned.

'Fairly grand,' she admitted truthfully. 'Privileged.'

He didn't say anything for a while, and then, when he

next spoke, his question was so unexpected that her eyes widened in surprise.

'What *exactly* did you and my sister communicate about? Obviously not about Natasha, despite the sudden urgent bond you felt when you discovered that she had been orphaned.'

Angela watched him warily as he said this, not quite knowing what was coming next, but suspecting that it was leading up to something.

'Oh, this and that,' she said vaguely. 'You know....'

'If I knew, I wouldn't have asked, would I?' His eyes were quite cold, the colour of sea in winter and as unfathomable.

'I don't understand why we have to keep returning to this,' she said stiffly, hoping to underwrite her unwelcoming tone of voice with a baffled but amicable enough smile.

'If you weren't so evasive, then there would be no mystery to solve, would there?'

He made things sound so reasonable, she thought, so *logical*. It was as though he was determined to pit his wits against hers and would not be satisfied until he emerged the winner. Just, no doubt, as he did in every other aspect of his life.

'There *is* no mystery,' Angela insisted. 'No ex-lover lurking in the background, waiting to stage a grand reunion. There's no need for you to worry that I'll just up and leave.' None whatsoever, she thought to herself.

He didn't say anything, but there was a brooding speculation in his eyes that was beginning to unnerve her.

'Did Amanda ever mention *me*?' he asked softly, just when she was starting to think that the conversation had been put to bed once and for all.

'No. Why should she?' She could almost hear him

thinking— So she never talked about her home life, she never mentioned her family. What the hell were all those conversations about? Conversations intimate enough to form a bond so strong that you'd abandon everything simply to become a glorified nanny to my niece.

'She didn't mention, perhaps, that I was rich? Unattached?' The accusation was phrased with such silky softness, steel in a velvet glove, that it took a few seconds for it to register. Then she felt her body stiffen and the colour drain from her face.

'What exactly are you trying to imply?'

'You know precisely what I'm implying. I can read it on your face.'

'That I engineered everything because I wanted an entry into your household? That I'm a gold-digger? That's the most ridiculous suggestion I've ever heard in my life.'

'Is it?' He looked at her coldly and she had to fight the temptation to squirm. He was completely off target, she had nothing to hide on that score, but she still felt uncomfortable—the way an innocent person sometimes felt uncomfortable in the presence of a policeman. 'You're a schoolteacher, paid enough to live on but not enough to really enjoy the finer things in life, and you're clearly not so enamoured of your job that you couldn't leave it at the drop of a hat. I've met enough gold-diggers in my time...'

'To have a completely jaundiced opinion of the opposite sex,' Angela finished for him. Her voice was as cold as his had been, and her hands were trembling so much that she sat on them. 'I hope you won't think me speaking out of turn if I tell you that I feel sorry for you. I can't imagine what it must be like to be suspicious of the whole world. Money must mean an awful lot to you if you think that every person you meet is waiting in the wings for a chance to take some of it away from you, that material greed fuels everyone's responses.'

She dropped her eyes, and then continued in a forced voice, 'I'm afraid I had to say that because I resent your accusation. We have to work together for Natasha's sake. We'll never be able to do that unless you at least give me the benefit of the doubt.'

They were at long last close to his office. She could recognise the glass building. He leaned forward and tapped on the partition and gave George instructions to collect him from work at seven-thirty. Then he relaxed back in his seat and turned to face her.

'I'll give you the benefit of the doubt—at least for the time being.' The car drew up outside the office and he opened the door, then said, over his shoulder, 'I just wanted to make sure that you knew how the ground lay. Tread carefully.'

Then he slammed the door behind him and was gone.

CHAPTER FOUR

'NATASHA, Mrs Pritchard asked to see me this morning after I dropped you off. She's concerned that you're not trying your hardest at school.' Mrs Pritchard was the class mistress, and this was a kind approximation of what had been said. 'Wilfully underachieving' had been the exact words, and they had been backed up by various exercise books which displayed a wide range of doodles in between half-finished work, sloppily done and in some cases aborted in mid-sentence.

Angela had not been surprised. For the past two weeks she had determinedly tried to break through Natasha's sullen defences and had been met with a brick wall. She had patiently sat down every evening with her after she had had her tea and had gone through exercise after exercise, trying to find out where her daughter's benchmark was and failing time after time.

Natasha was stunningly uninterested in anything to do with schoolwork and made no effort to disguise the fact.

'So?' Natasha asked now, scraping her food to one pile at the side of her plate and closing her knife and fork.

Angela looked at the downturned mouth and propped her chin on the palm of her hand.

It had been an uphill struggle all the way, but she wasn't even near to losing her temper. Even Natasha in a constant childish temper against the whole world was a feast to her eyes. Even though that mouth had not once smiled, Angela could picture the smile, like a ray of sunlight, and her imagination gave her a patience she had never known she had possessed.

She realised that she was settling into a routine of sorts. In the morning she drove Natasha off to school, a journey punctuated by one-sided conversation. During the day she prepared some work for Natasha to do after school, working on the premise that if she made the topics interesting enough, then some curiosity might be generated. A useless mission thus far. She also painted, much to her surprise, since that had only ever been a useful reason to give for willingly throwing in her teaching job. Even more to her surprise, she found that she rather enjoyed it. It was relaxing to do it for herself, rather than convert what talent she had into trying to teach the basics to mostly uninterested teenagers.

'So,' Angela said, 'I expect you've already been told that the one thing you owe yourself is a good education. I expect you've been told that you're lucky to be going to one of the best private schools in the country. That there are some children who have to fight against massive odds to get themselves educated.'

'Are you going to lecture to me?' Natasha asked suspiciously, but Angela thought it a promising sign that at least she was focusing on her face instead of staring somewhere else.

'Nope.' She stood up and began clearing the table. 'Where's the point?' she asked, with her back to Natasha.

'Good. Because you're right. There's no point. You're not my mother.'

Angela froze for a second, then continued with what she was doing.

'Not that *that* matters anyway,' Natasha said, in her

longest burst of conversation to date. 'She didn't care enough to keep me.'

Angela paused and looked at the child sitting at the table. There was beauty there, underneath the frowning, rebellious expression and the recalcitrant dark eyes.

She said, 'Come on. Upstairs. I'm going to paint you.'

'What?'

'You heard me. I'm going to paint you.' There would be time enough for Natasha to volunteer whatever information she wanted to, whatever buried grievances she had. Angela didn't think that she could pursue the topic now without going to pieces.

They went upstairs to the room she had set aside for her studio, in which Natasha had shown zero interest in seeing before, and as she arranged her into the right pose—chin in hands, face forward, hair slightly dishevelled—she felt the familiar sense of peace that always washed over her the minute she lifted her brush.

She put up the easel, fished out her paints and began. Quick sketches to start with, capturing the expression, the shape of the face, the stormy vulnerability in the eyes. She found that she was talking into the silent room and it was like talking to herself. She remembered bits of her childhood which she had forgotten, feelings that she had swept aside under the carpet, and Natasha, for once, was listening. Or maybe she just seemed to be, because she was held captive in her silent pose with no option.

It didn't matter. The time flew. She only realised how fast when there was a knock at the door and she glanced at her watch and saw that it was seven-thirty.

It was Nick. He stood at the doorway, elegantly formal in his business suit, and he was looking at the painting, what little she had accomplished so far, with such concentration that Angela suddenly felt embarrassed enough to want to put a cloth over it.

She had always felt exposed through her paintings, as though they might reveal something inside her that she didn't want the world to see.

'I've only just started,' she explained, reddening, while Natasha clambered off the chair and reluctantly went to join her uncle in his inspection.

'So, you really do paint,' he drawled, coming inside and unhurriedly strolling around the room, examining the few things she had done: some charcoal drawings, a still life, the view of trees from the window within a dull atmosphere of smog, so that the effect of a haven in the middle of a city was as plain as if she had painted buildings surrounding the garden.

'Of course I do!' Angela snapped. 'You didn't seriously think that I was fabricating a tissue of lies, did you?'

Natasha was following this exchange with an expression of surprise, and Angela got the feeling that she wasn't used to seeing her uncle spoken to as though he wasn't the demi-God that the world clearly saw him as being.

'I didn't think that you were this good,' he admitted, pausing to stand in front of the portrait of his niece. 'This is really impressive.'

Angela began to feel a little less nettled. 'I'm not terribly self-confident when it comes to portraits,' she admitted, moving to stand next to Natasha so that they were all looking at the easel as though examining some masterpiece from the Tate Gallery. 'And I have to confine myself to neck upwards only. I'm awful when it comes to hands and fingers.'

'So am I,' Natasha said shyly, then she blushed and resumed the sullen frown.

Angela felt as though a ray of brilliant sunshine had suddenly burst through a layer of cloud.

'I'm ready for bed,' Natasha announced, folding her arms, and Angela looked at her with incredulous surprise.

'Already!' she couldn't resist teasing. 'Where's your usual lecture about not having a bedtime?'

'Very funny,' Natasha muttered, but there was a shadow of a smile tugging the corners of her mouth.

Angela felt another great rush of joy. She wanted to dance round the room. Instead, she said briskly to Nick, 'Perhaps you could turn Natasha's covers back?'

Their eyes swivelled in unison to her and they both looked as though she had asked him to leap over the Niagara Falls in a barrel. The harsh, aggressive lines of Nick's face now displayed something suspiciously close to confusion, which made her want to laugh.

'I must get cleaned up.' She glanced expressively at her hands and the dabs of paint on her shirt, which would now have to join the bundle of 'painting clothes,' which she kept purely for the purpose of being able to get them dirty without any attendant guilt. 'Would you mind?' she asked innocently, and Nick looked at her with quick, appreciative amusement in his grey eyes.

'Of course not,' he murmured, lifting his eyebrows. 'Do we mind, Natasha?' he asked, and she gazed at him with sudden humour on her face. It gave her such lively prettiness that Angela had to look away with a lump in her throat, and she could see from Nick's expression that he was as stunned at the change as she was.

'What if we did?' Natasha asked with a wicked, side-long glance. 'What choice would we have? She'd only give us detention. She *is* a schoolteacher after all.'

She exited the room, and Nick turned and grinned at Angela over his shoulder. For a brief fraction of a second she felt as though she had had the rug pulled from under her, then he was gone as well, and she dashed to her bedroom and cleaned up, feeling terribly happy all of a sudden.

Don't, she told herself sternly, changing into a pair of jeans and a white shirt. Don't think that this marks the beginning of anything. Natasha will be her usual self in the morning and then you'll only feel sick and disappointed. And Nick, she thought, Nick is still suspicious of you and will continue to be because he's clever enough to know that there's something not quite right about you being here. You still have to watch out and walk very carefully when he's around, not become muddle-headed just because he flashes a smile in your direction.

But she was still feeling foolishly muddle-headed fifteen minutes later, when she strolled into the sitting room with a cup of coffee. She couldn't seem to help herself.

'You look very pleased with yourself.'

Angela hadn't expected to find anyone there, so Philippa's voice had the effect of a bucket of cold water being poured onto her from a great height. She stopped dead in her tracks and stared at the woman who was sitting in a chair by the window, elegant in an emerald-green suit which gave her the sinewy beauty of something tigerish and ever so slightly disturbing.

'I'm sorry,' Angela stammered, 'I didn't expect to find...'

'Me here?' Philippa finished for her. She crossed her legs and linked her fingers on her lap. They were impeccably polished in deep red. Blood-red, Angela thought uncharitably. 'Nick dropped by to change. We're on our way out.' She smiled and didn't enlarge on that, so that

Angela was left with the impression that the evening was something so intimate that the details could hardly be mentioned to her.

'Were you doing your childminding duties?' Philippa asked, and Angela nodded, annoyed at the description even though there was nothing overtly rude about it. Just enough of a hint of the patronising to set her teeth on edge.

'And how are you finding it? A challenge, I expect.' She laughed and Angela bared her teeth in a polite smile. She dwelled on the passing fantasy of flinging her cup of coffee at the emerald-green suit and was left with pleasant visions of indelible brown stains and a massive crack in that icy cold composure. Shame, she thought, that it *was* just a passing fantasy. She took a sip of coffee and edged towards a chair.

'Very enjoyable.'

'Good.' Philippa paused and then continued, smiling, 'And how do you like living in the same house as Nick?'

'I beg your pardon?'

'I asked how you liked living here, in this house, with Nick.' The green eyes narrowed but the mouth was still set in a smile.

'I don't see much of him,' Angela said, bemused. 'I gather he works very late.'

'Mmm. He *is* out until late at night,' Philippa laughed huskily. 'Lucky for you, I guess. Well, for both of you!'

'What do you mean?'

'I mean,' she said, and looked down at her nails, examining them thoroughly before raising her eyes to Angela's face, 'that darling Nick does tend to make a habit of attracting the opposite sex, and it occurred to me that, living in such close quarters with him, as you are, you might just find yourself becoming one of his adoring fans…'

'So you're warning me off?'

'Woman to woman. It's so easy to get hurt when you're attracted to a man who doesn't know that you exist.'

'I expect it is.'

'Normally I wouldn't mention this, but, the situation being what it is, it would put him in quite an awkward position…'

'Thanks for the advice,' Angela said coldly. The image of the flying cup of coffee moved from passing fantasy to distinct possibility, and she deposited her cup on the table next to her, to remove temptation from easy reach.

'Not that you really need it,' Philippa hastened to add. 'I mean, it's hardly as though you're his type and vice versa, is it?' She clearly expected some kind of response to this, because she left a long pause which Angela sat through in tight-lipped silence.

'He's terribly single-minded in the kind of woman he likes,' Philippa confided after a while, sitting forward as though imparting a sisterly confidence. Angela could tell that she was niggled at the lack of response, though, because her eyes were bright and cold and she was no longer bothering to smile.

'I'm not very interested in the kind of…'

'Men are very much creatures of habit, aren't they? Have you noticed? They always go for the same type. I'd say that Nick's attracted to glamour with a capital G. I guess that's why…' She laughed her throaty laugh and let the insinuation dangle in the air, and at the sound of approaching footsteps they both stood up.

Nick came in, his grey eyes flitting between the two of them. Seeing what? Angela thought. A bare-faced blonde, with her hair in a ponytail and most of the paint scrubbed off her fingers but still a little left under her fingernails, wearing jeans and a baggy man's white shirt. And a raven-haired, green-eyed witch, dressed in *haute couture*, who had probably never been near a pot of paint in her entire life. Glamour, as she had tacitly described herself, with a capital G.

'Ready, Philippa?' he asked, while Angela hovered with her arms folded, feeling like a teenager at an adult gathering.

'Sure am!' Philippa moved towards him and turned to Angela with a smile. 'So nice to have met you again. I can just *feel* that you're going to do a world of good for Natasha!'

'I hope so.' She knew that Nick was looking at her, sensing an atmosphere. She also knew that if she glanced in his direction she would feel destabilised, so she kept her eyes firmly averted from his face and resorted to the age-old trick of focusing on nothing at all, so that Philippa became little more than a background colour. A moving shrub of some sort. All that green.

She stayed in the sitting room until she heard the front door slam, then tentatively ventured out to the kitchen and sat thoughtfully at the table and ate the salad which Eva had meticulously made for her earlier.

So this is what it feels like to be warned off a man, she thought. It left a bitter aftertaste. Now she could list thousands of things she might have said at the time, cutting yet witty repartee which would have left Philippa gasping for air. It made the blood rush to her head to think how she had just sat there, semi-mute.

If only Philippa knew. If only *both* of them knew the real reason for her presence here.

Philippa would never have issued those veiled threats

and Nick would never have made the insulting accusation that she had inveigled herself into his household because she had somehow found out how much he was worth.

And Natasha. Natasha, she thought, with a sigh, would hate her.

She finished the salad, washed her plate and cutlery, and checked on Natasha, who was sleeping the sleep of the innocent, but she couldn't go to sleep herself. She lay there until she heard the sound of a car outside, the opening and shutting of the front door, and when she checked the clock by her bed, she saw that it was after one in the morning.

It would never do. She had applied for this job for a purpose and she wasn't going to get side-tracked into a tangled web of emotion.

For the next week she made sure that she only saw Nick in passing—on her way out of the kitchen, or the sitting room, or whatever room he happened to be entering at the time. In fact, she thought that she was becoming rather adept at the 'departing visitor' routine.

It didn't bother her at all that her avoidance tactics were beginning to get on his nerves. One night she had genuinely been about to leave the sitting room and head for bed at nine-thirty, when he had walked in and said, with heavy sarcasm, 'On your way out, are you?'

'Yes, I am,' Angela had said, smiling, and had met a frown in response.

'Shall I make an appointment to see you some time, so that we can discuss my niece?' he had asked, pouring himself a drink and turning to look at her over the rim of the glass.

'Any time you want to discuss Natasha, I should be only to happy to oblige,' she had said with another vague smile.

'In that case, what about now?' he had bellowed. 'Sit down! And stay seated! I don't want to feel that I have to nail you to the chair to keep you there!'

So she had obediently sat and talked about Natasha's progress, of which there had been some. Natasha was actually responding in more than her usual sulky monosyllables, and there had been two more smiles. Angela thought that she found their painting sessions, which had developed into a regular forty-minute sitting every evening before bed, as therapeutic as she did.

'Well,' Nick had said drily, after he had listened to her account, 'you seem to be achieving more in a few weeks than I ever did in several months.'

'Is that all?' Angela had asked, edging off her chair, and he had slammed his glass on the table in front of him.

'Why? Have you got exciting plans ahead of you? At—' he had looked at his watch '—nine-thirty in the evening? If so, I'm dying to hear what they are!'

'Just sleep.' She had yawned expressively. 'I'm awfully tired.'

'In that case, I mustn't keep you, must I?' he had asked with cold irritation, which she had ignored, proffering another flashing smile.

But what else, she thought now, could he have said? He could hardly *force* her to stay and chat to him, could he? And she wasn't going to volunteer her company. If he needed company, he had the gorgeous Philippa, whom she had just managed to avoid seeing two days ago. She had appeared with him at the house in the evening, when Angela and Natasha had been in the kitchen, doing homework together, and Angela had conveniently excused herself to go to the bathroom just as she'd heard footsteps approaching. She didn't really care whose footsteps they were. She had no inclination to see either Nick or his girlfriend.

A bit treacherous, she had thought guiltily, leaving Natasha to face them on her own, but she had still been relieved when she had returned to the kitchen twenty minutes later to discover that they had gone.

These thoughts flashed through her head like action replays in a movie as she stood now, in front of the easel, applying paint in small, delicate strokes to the portrait taking shape in front of her.

'Natasha,' she said, looking at the girl, 'keep still. You're fidgeting.'

'I'm bored and my feet have got pins and needles.'

Angela sighed to herself. It was the first time Natasha had mentioned being bored since the sessions had begun, and she hoped that the sulkiness wasn't about to resurface.

'Wriggle your toes,' she said, 'and that might stop you getting bored. Who knows? It might even do something for the pins and needles.'

'Ha-ha,' Natasha said, with her mouth downturned so that Angela was obliged to stop painting completely. 'I don't see the point of continuing with this anyway.' Her voice was petulant and oddly unsteady.

'I thought you enjoyed it.'

'What if I do?' Natasha looked at her with sullen challenge in her eyes. 'It's not going to last, is it? Nothing ever does.' Her mouth quivered, and Angela stood completely still. To go over and comfort her would be a mistake. She would be shrugged off, and any chance of finding out what this was all about would be lost.

'I don't know what you're talking about,' she said calmly, and Natasha threw her a furious, teary-eyed frown.

'Yes, you do. You've been plotting with that awful woman!' Her voice had risen a couple of decibels and was bordering on the hysterical.

'What awful woman?'

'Philippa I-love-myself Ames! That's who! And don't deny it! She told me.'

'She told you *what*?'

Natasha was stoically trying to avoid a crying fit by sniffing a lot and glaring. Angela went over and stood next to her, thinking how urgently she wanted to throw her arms around her, tuck that childish face into the crook of her neck and stroke her hair and soothe whatever troubles were bothering her.

'What did she tell you?' she asked gently.

'That you've mentioned that I should be sent away to a boarding-school.'

There was stunned silence while Angela digested this remark. She could feel her heart plummeting downwards, followed by a burst of fury so intense that the blood rushed to her head. She felt giddy with it.

'Uncle Nick agrees too,' Natasha flung at her. 'He's never wanted me.'

'Boarding-school? Boarding-school? That is the most preposterous suggestion I have ever heard in my life.' She reached out and held Natasha's hands very firmly in her own. 'Over my dead body,' she said in a flat, hard voice, and Natasha raised her eyes uncertainly to hers.

'I don't want to be sent away,' she said, in such a low voice that Angela had to lean forward to hear.

'You're right there,' she muttered forcefully. 'You're *not* going to be sent anywhere. Trust me.'

'Why should I?'

'Because I'm asking you to,' she said, which seemed to have a calming effect. They returned to the painting but Angela couldn't concentrate. She looked at the canvas and saw Nick and Philippa, heads bent together over some intimate, candlelit dinner, making plans to send *her* daughter away from her. *Her daughter!* Her whole reason for living.

She went through the routine of putting Natasha to bed, then had a long bath, slipped on a pair of leggings and a shirt, and went to the sitting room to wait for Nick to get back. She didn't care if she had to stay there until midnight.

At ten-thirty she heard his car, and she sprang to her feet and was waiting for him the minute he entered the house. He looked at her, dropped his briefcase on the ground and slowly shut the door. Then he turned and stared at her unsmilingly with his arms folded.

'What a warm welcome,' he drawled. 'Like being greeted by a rattlesnake.'

'I want to have a word with you.'

'Can it wait until tomorrow? I've had a bloody hard day at work and I just want to go to sleep.'

'No,' Angela said flatly, 'it cannot wait until tomorrow, and I don't care if you're dead on your feet.'

'Is that so?' he asked coldly. He began walking up the stairs, removing his jacket on the way and undoing his tie. She followed him in his wake, furiously determined to have this matter out if she had to lock them into his bedroom.

Which was a very brave thought at the bottom of the stairs, but about halfway up she began to feel the first stirrings of hesitancy, and by the time they entered his bedroom her heart felt somewhere between her ribcage and her feet.

She had never ventured anywhere near his bedroom before. It was on the third floor of the house, and was more of a suite than a bedroom, impeccably furnished like the rest of the house, but with a rich, very masculine feel to it.

He walked into the bedroom and began stripping off his shirt, and she said with ice in her voice, 'Do you mind? I want to have a conversation with you. I don't particularly want to see you do a striptease.'

'You followed me up here. I intend to have a shower. If that bothers you, then feel free to leave and we'll discuss this at a more civilised hour tomorrow evening. If not, then go ahead and say what you have to say.'

He was now half-naked, and disconcertingly well-built. His arms were lean and strong, with the muscles rippling under sinewy skin. Angela stood by the door, nervously wondering whether she *should* just leave and confront him the following evening. But then she thought of Natasha's quivering lip, the fear in her eyes at the prospect of being sent away to a boarding-school. She thought of her own fear of being deprived of her daughter for the second time and she resolutely stood her ground. Let him damn well undress. If he thought that he could embarrass her into leaving, then he was wrong. She had seen a naked man before, albeit so long ago that it seemed in another life.

He unbuckled his belt and pulled it out in one easy movement, then he began unzipping his trousers, at which point she felt her heart begin to race and turned away to stare at the wall.

'Natasha informed me this evening that you and your girlfriend have raised the suggestion of sending her to a boarding-school.'

'Oh, yes?'

She wasn't looking at his face so she couldn't see his expression, but there was a soft wariness in his voice which she immediately translated into agreement with what she had said.

'"Oh, yes", indeed,' she snapped. 'And I want to know if it's true!'

'I take it that you don't go along with the idea,' he said calmly, neither agreeing nor disagreeing with her demand. She heard the sound of his trousers being tossed into the corner of the room to join the shirt, then he vanished towards the bathroom.

After a decent enough interval she followed suit, to find that he hadn't even bothered to half shut the door. It was wide open, and before she could look somewhere else she saw him in the shower, a tall, muscular shape behind the cloudy doors of the cubicle. And, of course, once her eyes were on him, she found it impossible to tear them away.

She had lived a life too deprived of the opposite sex, she told herself shakily. Ever since Simon, she had had a deep distrust of them and had avoided them meticulously, never allowing them to go beyond the boundaries of non-threatening friendship. What that meant, she thought, was that this sudden intimate situation in which she now found herself was unsettling her way beyond what it should have done.

When he turned off the shower and opened the door to get his towel, which he had slung on the floor, she turned away with such speed that she nearly fell over. She had forgotten what they had been talking about. Images of his naked body had sent her thoughts flying to all four winds.

'You employed me to look after Natasha, and—' she began, ignoring the sounds of him drying.

'You can look at me now. I'm quite decent.'

She slid her eyes across to him and saw that the towel

was wrapped round the lower half of his body. His hair was still damp and there were droplets of water on his face. He didn't look 'quite decent'. Not at all.

'Are you as coy as this with all men or just with me?'

'I am not here to discuss myself,' Angela said frostily, to cover her gauche embarrassment. 'As I was saying, you employed me to look after your niece, and I feel quite angry that decisions such as whether or not to send her to boarding-school should be made without any thought of consulting me.' She wondered whether that sounded arrogant and decided that she didn't care.

'Why do you think that she wouldn't benefit from a boarding-school atmosphere?' He wasn't bothering to get dressed. He stood in front of her without a trace of embarrassment at his semi-nudity.

Angela felt that rush of fury again and stuck her hands on her hips. Her face was going red. She could feel it burning, tingling.

'What she needs is the comfort of people around her who *care*. I know that she's disrupted your life and that it would probably be easier for you if she weren't around, but, whether you like it or not, you have a responsibility to Natasha! I also fail to see what input your girlfriend should have in deciding the future of *your* niece!' And *my daughter*, she wanted to yell at him.

'Why do you keep referring to Philippa as my *girl-friend?*' was all he asked.

'Why do you keep refusing to answer my questions?' she shouted at him.

'I have no idea why this subject of boarding-school has cropped up,' he said calmly. 'You launch yourself at me, full of fury, but Philippa has certainly not discussed anything of the sort with me. I, personally, am more than pleased with how you're coping with my niece.'

'She hasn't?' Angela asked dumbly. 'You are?'

'She hasn't. I am. Natasha's the most relaxed that she's been since the accident. You probably can't see that because you don't have the element of comparison that I have, but trust me when I tell you that she is. Why would I even consider sending her to a boarding-school under those circumstances?'

She didn't know what to say. She had geared herself up for a long, confrontational argument and now she felt a little winded.

She also, suddenly and dramatically, became aware of the fact that he had no clothes on. It had bothered her before, but she had had so much on her mind that she had turned a blind eye to the intimacy of their situation.

She took a couple of steps back, folding her arms protectively in front of her, and said coolly, 'You might have said all this from the start, instead of letting me...' make a fool of myself, she finished silently.

'I might have,' he agreed, moving towards her so imperceptibly that she was hardly aware of it until she found that he was standing right in front of her once again. 'But I was curious to know why you were so emotional over the possibility of Natasha leaving. Was it just a question of finding yourself out of a job?'

Uncomfortably Angela muttered something about seeing a task through.

'Also, I have to admit that I was intrigued by the change in you from sensible prim schoolteacher to fiery young woman.' He smiled very slowly and continued looking at her, and she felt thousands of odd little vibrations begin to ripple through her body.

'It—it wasn't my intention to appear fiery,' she stammered, trying to recover some of that sensible, schoolteacherish primness that he had mentioned. 'I merely wanted to discuss…'

'In a very loud voice,' he said lazily, 'with blazing eyes…'

'I apologise if…'

'Why?' His voice was curious, amused, soft. 'I like the show of fire.' He reached out, still looking down into her eyes, and coiled his long fingers into her hair.

To be touched by a man… For the first time in so many years…. Her head told her how she should react, that she should draw back with fear and disgust—a legacy of Simon—but she couldn't obey her head at the moment. What she felt was neither fear nor disgust, but a strange, exciting, primitive tingle of anticipation that made her body freeze and her breathing quicken.

Her eyes felt drowsy. Was he going to kiss her? His lips were so close to hers…

CHAPTER FIVE

IT SEEMED an eternity between that passing, nebulous speculation and the touch of his mouth against hers, even though it could only have been a matter of seconds.

Her mind went completely blank. She pressed the palms of her hands against his chest, still cool and damp, and moaned softly as his lips moved over hers and his tongue invaded the softness of her mouth. He was gentle, persuasive, but firmly insistent, and as she responded unthinkingly to his deepening kiss she felt his hunger begin to grow, until he was pressing her against him, one hand on the small of her back, the other still curled into her hair, tugging her head back to accommodate his questing mouth.

She was burning up inside. Some tiny flame had been ignited and now seemed to be devouring her like an inferno. Her breathing was fast and jerky, and became even more so when his mouth moved from hers to lick and nibble the column of her neck. She knew that she was moaning but the sound appeared to be coming from far away, not from *her*. Her legs felt shaky, and when he lifted her off her feet and carried her across to his bed she didn't protest. She was being dragged into a vortex where time and thought no longer mattered.

Very slowly, and still with his mouth against her neck, he began unbuttoning her shirt. That, too, seemed to take an eternity. She was so hot! She needed cool air on her breasts. He pulled the shirt free and instead of unclasping her bra, which would have been an awkward manoeuvre because the clasp was at the back, he simply shoved the lacy material up so that her breasts were exposed.

She heard him groan and then his hand covered her breast and she shuddered convulsively. She arched back, thrusting her body upwards, and he played with her nipples, which were hard and erect, teasing them with his fingers, rolling the swollen nubs with his thumbs until she wanted to scream.

Her face was flushed with a sort of exquisite, liberating pleasure, her mouth half parted, her eyes closed. When he licked the tip of one nipple she sighed and writhed and clasped her fingers in his hair, pushing his head down harder so that he was sucking wetly against her breast, drawing her aching nipple into his mouth while his tongue seemed to make direct contact with nerve-endings that sent darts of sensual pleasure through her.

His hand moved down the flat plane of her stomach and she automatically parted her legs. She wanted to kick off her leggings. They felt like weights of lead against her.

She was hardly aware of him pulling them down, then his hand slid beneath her cotton underwear to find the dampness between her thighs, and his finger moved, exploring rhythmically, stroking and rubbing, while his mouth found her other breast so that the physical sensations were washing over every part of her body.

She was dimly aware that she had lost herself completely, that she couldn't summon up enough coherent thought to find her way out again. She was in a room without doors and not even certain that she wanted to find one.

It was only when he drew her onto her side, so that

her body was against his, and guided her hand towards his arousal, that all the common sense which had deserted her flooded back like a tidal wave of crashing, icy water.

She remembered Simon. His face flew into her mind, lewd, smiling, cruel, the face of a stranger, and then she was bombarded by all the fright and dismay that she had felt then.

She jack-knifed away from Nick, scrabbling until she was off the bed, tugging at her clothes in a desperate attempt to get them back where they belonged, which was covering her body. She was trembling, and when he stood up and walked towards her she began backing away in panic.

How could she have responded like that? Had it been the suddenness of his seduction? Except it hadn't been *that* sudden, had it? She had followed him up to his bedroom, she had stood blindly there while he showered, too intent on confronting him to see the danger signals waving over her head like great red banners. And she had known his intention to kiss her even before his mouth had descended. Humiliation joined all the other emotions raging through her, and when he gripped her arms and shook her she couldn't bring herself to look at him.

'What the hell is the matter?' he asked. 'Look at me!'

She continued to fiddle with the buttons on her shirt, until he grasped her hands in his and pulled them down to her sides.

'What's wrong?' he demanded in a low, urgent voice.

'I want you to leave me alone! I don't understand what came over me...I just want you to leave me alone.'

'You understand as well as I do!' he grated.

But she really didn't. She had accepted for years that something inside her had died a long time ago, some

ability to respond to the opposite sex. How had she suc-
cumbed to Nick Cameron with such abandon?

'That should never have happened,' she whispered.

'It's irrelevant speculating on whether or not it should
have happened. The fact is that it did, and what I want
to know is why you suddenly pulled back. And look at
me when I'm trying to talk to you!'

Angela looked at him, and winced at the angry incom-
prehension on his face.

'Look, can we just forget that this ever happened?' she
asked timidly. 'It's my fault. I accept that. I shouldn't
have followed you up here. I wanted to talk, but I should
have waited. I realise that now.' But she had never seriously imagined that he would make a pass at her, however intimate the situation, and she had imagined even
less that she would respond to him the way that she had.

'Why did you pull back?'

'Stop asking me that!' she told him in a high voice. 'I
did and that's all there is to it!'

'I don't like women who play games,' he grated
harshly, and she looked at him in utter confusion.

'Games? What games? What are you talking about?'

'You know exactly what I'm talking about, so you can
wipe that butter-wouldn't-melt-in-my-mouth expression
from your face! You're not a naïve child! That's apparent
from the way you responded to me!' His fingers tightened
on her wrists, hurting her. She wished that he would let
her go. She wanted to run away, and if it hadn't been for
Natasha, she would have done just that—run as far away
from him as she could and as fast as possible. He had
unleashed something in her and she didn't understand
how he had managed to do it. But she knew that it was
dangerous.

'I don't know what you're saying,' she insisted in a miserable whisper.

'What did you hope to gain by leading me on and then freezing over like a block of ice at the last minute?' His mouth curled into an unpleasant sneer. 'Do you imagine that playing hard to get will turn you into someone I can't resist?'

'Of course not!' Angela denied hotly. 'And I wasn't playing hard to get! I just changed my mind... I couldn't...' But she knew how it must look to him. She had not once murmured a word of resistance. She had let him touch her in the most intimate way possible and then she had leapt off the bed and acted like a distraught virgin. He had jumped to the obvious conclusion because he was completely ignorant of what had motivated her behaviour, and, since she wasn't going to enlighten him, he would just have to assume the worst.

'I should ask you to hand in your notice,' he said, letting her go and strolling across the room to wrap the towel back around his waist.

She didn't want to, but Angela followed him with her eyes, unable to resist her fascination with his body, and she felt her own body stir once again, with a response that bewildered her this time, and frightened her. It was as if her own body was trying to tell her something, except her brain couldn't quite grasp the message.

She dragged her attention away, and when the meaning of what he had just said sank in she began to tremble in shock.

'I mean,' he continued smoothly and coldly, 'after what's happened, we can hardly have much of a working relationship, can we?'

'Please don't ask me to leave,' she said in a stifled

voice. 'I know that I was to blame and I promise you that it won't happen again.'

'I never said that you were to blame.' He looked at her narrowly, his eyes hard. 'But you *do* agree that what's happened might make things a little awkward between us?'

'We don't tend to see one another regularly,' Angela said, finding the first objection she could think of and latching onto it for dear life. 'If I worked for you in some other capacity—if I worked at your office, perhaps, and we saw each other for hours on end—then perhaps, yes. But I only really need to see you in passing. I mean, we could feasibly not cross paths for weeks on end!'

'And when we do?'

Angela shrugged and tried to look as experienced and as nonchalant as she could. 'We could consign it to the past. A mistake. They happen.'

'Oh, yes, they certainly do, don't they?'

'Yes!' she said eagerly. Another lifebelt in the offing. All she had to do was imply that as a woman of the world she could easily forget the unfortunate little incident. He must mix in circles where women did that all the time. Sleep with men—which thankfully she hadn't, so it wasn't as though she had *that* much to relegate to the past, was it?—and then casually move on without a backward glance.

'This sort of thing happens to you quite frequently, does it?' he asked blandly, raising his eyebrows as though considering the question for the first time.

'I never said that.'

'But you implied it.'

Angela greeted this with silence.

'Which brings me to an interesting point. If you're so experienced that you have no problem dismissing what happened between us, then how is it that you'd have me believe that you suddenly fell victim to last minute scruples? Do experienced women generally tend to suffer from last minute scruples?' He appeared to give this some thought as well, but she knew that he wasn't really thinking about it. He was building a trap in the hope that she would fall in.

There was further silence, since she couldn't think of anything to say to that. She was also beginning to feel annoyed at the methodical way he was cornering her, as though the blame for what had happened lay firmly on her shoulders. True, she had made a point of accepting it, but he wasn't exactly exempt, was he? Even if she hadn't resisted, it was still he who had made the first move.

'Are you annoyed with me because you've never been refused by a woman before?' she asked recklessly, and his mouth thinned. 'Look,' she hurried on placatingly, 'Natasha and I are really beginning to get to know one another and I think it would be foolish for me to leave over something as silly as what happened. I think she needs stability in her life just now and—'

'What if it happens again?' he asked curiously, and a shiver ran through her. What was he saying? That he was attracted to her? Or was this leading up to another trick question out of which she would have difficulty manoeuvring herself?

'It won't!' she promised fervently.

'How can you be so sure?' He asked that as though they were discussing something quite interesting but purely theoretical.

'Because basically you're not my type any more than I'm yours.' She thought of Philippa and hung onto the thought tenaciously. It helped to convince her of the absolute accuracy of that statement—which circumstances seemed to undermine the minute she started examining it in too much depth.

'And what *is* your type?'

Angela thought quickly about a type. She didn't *have* a type, but saying that, she knew, would not be the most diplomatic of answers.

'Short.' She folded her arms and frowned. 'Short and average-looking, I guess. Maybe with spectacles.'

'A short, nondescript, bespectacled man?' He laughed as though he found the thought of that highly amusing.

'Yes. They *do* exist, you know.'

'Yes, I know that.' He began dressing, pulling on a short-sleeved shirt, then rummaging through his wardrobe until he found a pair of trousers, which he proceeded to don without the slightest sign of inhibition. An experienced woman would have calmly watched this process without batting an eye, but Angela shifted her gaze away discreetly.

'Well,' he continued, shoving his hands in his trouser pockets and smiling in an infuriatingly amused way, 'I just want you to know that I feel absolutely in agreement that nothing will happen between us since you're attracted to men who are diametrically opposed to me.'

She nodded and eyed the door. 'So, would it be correct for me to assume that my employment here hasn't been terminated?'

'Oh, yes, I think so. You're quite right. You're good for my niece and I certainly have no desire to deprive her of that when her life has already suffered enough upheaval.'

Angela felt a lot of the tension leave her. 'Thank you,' she said, smiling genuinely for the first time. 'Your confidence in me won't be misplaced.' She turned towards the door, aware that he was walking after her.

'Tell me one more thing,' he murmured into her ear, and she froze and stared at her feet.

'What?'

'What do you think is *my type* of woman?'

She shrugged, but he wasn't about to let her get away with her usual retreat into silence.

'You can't make sweeping generalisations without expanding on them,' he told her. 'Can you?'

I most certainly can, she thought to herself. 'Glamorous,' she said, without flinching. 'Expensive, sophisticated, urbane, glamorous women. Like Philippa Ames.'

'Like Philippa Ames. Did you get that general picture from her, by the way?' There was a hint of hardness in his voice that made her wonder uneasily whether she had said the wrong thing.

'No,' Angela said vaguely. 'No, I just sort of put two and two together and got four. Look, would you mind very much if I went to bed now?'

'Feel free.'

Released from the claustrophobia of his presence, she suddenly felt a deep reluctance to go back to her own bedroom. Too much adrenaline still flowing in her bloodstream, she told herself. Too many thoughts that made her head spin.

She walked away without a backward glance, even though she could feel his eyes on her as she descended the winding staircase that led from the top floor to the body of the house.

With some surprise, she found her eyes closed the minute her head hit the pillow.

It was a deep, dreamless sleep. So deep, in fact, that when she awoke the following morning she wondered whether she hadn't dreamt what had happened the night before. She lay on the bed with her eyes closed and immediately knew that it had been no dream—because the details of their lovemaking bombarded her with such force that she opened her eyes very quickly and got up, relying on hurried activity to dispel the memories.

Then she slunk like an intruder down to the kitchen, relieved to find that only Natasha was there, half-heartedly eating a bowl of cereal.

'Good news,' she said brightly.

Natasha looked at her warily.

'A smile in return for the good news?'

Natasha grimaced.

'OK. The good news is that I spoke to your uncle last night and there's to be no boarding-school.'

That didn't meet with the expected explosion of delight, and Angela sat down opposite her and cupped her face in the palm of her hand. 'I thought you'd be happy.'

'How do you know that you can believe him?' Natasha asked, ignoring that remark. She circled the spoon in what remained of the cereal, until Angela got up and removed it to the sink and returned to the table.

'Why shouldn't I believe him?' she asked, perplexed.

'Because he's considered it before.'

'He has?' She sat up abruptly. 'When?'

'A couple of months after I went to live with him in New York.' She shrugged defensively, even though Angela hadn't uttered a word. 'He didn't like having me around and neither did Philippa. I think Philippa started it, but Uncle Nick went along. He only backed out at the last minute because the school psychologist said that it'd be bad for me.'

'Why would Philippa have been bothered about

whether you went to a boarding-school or not?' Angela asked, knowing the answer before the question was even out.

Natasha looked at her with a sulky frown. 'Why d'you think?'

'Oh.' Because Natasha had been in the way. A difficult child, too old to be put to bed with a bottle of milk, too young to get wrapped up in parties with teenage friends, desperately needing attention. 'Well,' she said brightly, 'your uncle has told me that there's no such possibility and I think he's telling the truth. Let's be honest,' she carried on thoughtfully, 'if he intended sending you to a boarding-school, he would say so. He's not the sort of man who takes the easy route out by lying.'

'I suppose not,' Natasha conceded reluctantly. She looked a little relieved, which Angela supposed was the closest she would get to happy.

'And if he dares suggest it,' she said, 'he'll find himself with a fight on his hands.'

Natasha's eyes slipped up to meet Angela's and this time she did smile, but only for a second, then she stood up and it was business as usual.

'Oh, by the way,' she said as she was opening the car door to go into school, 'this is for you.' She rummaged around in her school folder and extracted a fairly mangled piece of paper—an invitation to the parents' evening.

Angela looked at her with amusement. 'How long have you had this?' she asked. 'It looks as though it's seen better days.'

Natasha blushed. 'A few days, maybe a week.'

'And appropriately you remembered one day before the event.'

Natasha shrugged and looked sheepish. 'I know what they're going to say anyway.'

'You might be surprised.'

'Will you go?' Natasha asked hesitantly, looking away into the distance, and Angela felt a pang of love.

'Your uncle…' she forced herself to say the words '…should be the one—'

'I don't want him to go. He'll just come back home and fly at me for not trying hard enough. It's happened before.'

'OK,' Angela told the averted profile. 'I'll go. But I still think that you'll be surprised. Your work's very good now and you haven't been leaving anything half-finished.'

'Really?' The expression was one of uninterest but the voice held childish pleasure at the compliment, and on the spur of the moment Angela leaned across and gave her a quick hug.

She felt a warm, deep surge of love, stronger because it had been denied for years. She would have liked to cling, but after a while she detached herself and said, for all the world as though nothing had happened. 'Have a good day at school, Natasha, and I'll be back here for you at four. *Promptly*, if you please! So less after-school dawdling!'

'OK, OK!' Natasha laughed, and once again Angela was stunned at the transformation of her face. 'See you later, and…' she got out of the car and looked back in '…thanks.'

One small word but it kept her on a high for the remainder of the day, and by the time Nick returned from work, at nine-thirty, she was still in a pleasant, mellow mood. Pleasant enough for her not to be daunted by the prospect of seeing him—which she intended to. She was beginning to know his habits by now. Heaven only knew what he did for food, but he rarely ate at home. Usually he would discard his jacket and head for the sitting room, where he would have a nightcap followed by more work or else the newspapers. He seemed to read them all, from the *Financial Times* to the *Guardian*.

Normally, the minute she heard him approaching, she would spring out of her chair and head for the door in her I'm-just-on-my-way-out mode, but now she remained where she was until he entered, and she could tell from his slight hesitation that he was startled to see her sitting there, legs curled underneath her.

I'm not going to mention what happened, she thought, but seeing him turned the tap on, and images of his body, lean and hard and aroused, flashed through her mind, joined by other, just as powerful memories, of her own body responding to him, on fire. She hoped that he would take the cue from her and say nothing about the night before, and sure enough he didn't, but she could tell from the coolness in his voice when he spoke that he hadn't consigned their mistake to regrettable experience.

'Can I get you a drink?' he asked politely, pouring himself one and turning around to face her.

Angela looked at the hard, unsmiling angles of his face and shook her head. 'I've just had a cup of coffee.' Pause. Where was that feeling of mellowness and everything's all-right-with-the-world? 'Actually, I wanted to talk to you about Natasha.'

'Again?' He strolled over to a chair and sat down. 'Not about this boarding-school business, I hope.' He swallowed a mouthful of his drink and looked at her over the rim of the glass. He continued looking at her after he had rested the glass on the coffee-table next to him and linked his fingers on his lap. 'I thought we had put that one to bed last night. Or perhaps I'm just confusing the topic with ourselves.'

Angela went red. What was it about this man that made it so difficult for her to maintain her composure in his presence? Presumably the same thing that had aroused such bewildering feelings of longing in her the night before. Some dark, persuasive quality that emanated from him and seemed to reach up and grab her by the throat.

'It's Parents' Night tomorrow evening,' she said levelly. 'I'm sorry about the short notice, but Natasha's only just given me the slip of paper.'

'I might as well tell you that the last one I went to was hardly a roaring success.'

'Was that at her present school?'

'New York,' he said. 'I informed them that they were inadequate and virtually incompetent if they couldn't deal with an eight-year-old child, albeit one suffering from some emotional trauma. I'm afraid they became rather defensive.' He crossed his legs and had another sip of his drink. 'It's possible that I lack the necessary tact to accept what I'm being told when I can see for myself that people are underachieving with my niece. It might be an idea if you went along on your own.'

'I think not,' Angela replied calmly. 'You *are*, in case you've forgotten, her guardian, and you'll be expected to take an interest in how she's coming along.'

'Of course I take an interest in how she's coming along,' he said with a hint of impatience.

'Good. In that case it starts at seven-thirty. I realise that you may have to leave work a little early, but I don't see how it can be helped. I did telephone to find out whether the appointment could be shifted back a bit, but all the later slots have been taken.'

They looked at each other and Angela made a point

of not looking away. Besides, she felt fine discussing this; it was impersonal, work-orientated, and there was enough physical distance between them to ensure that her pulses remained steady and her brain actually functioned.

'I also feel,' she continued in her much-used teacher's voice, 'that I should mention to you that Natasha has informed me that the last time you saw her teacher, be that in New York or whatever, you flew off the handle with her over what had been said.'

'I don't think that "flew off the handle" is precisely the right description. I just sat her down and told her that she was doing herself no favours in allowing herself to treat school as though it was something distasteful that had to be endured with the minimum amount of effort.'

'So in other words you flew off the handle.'

He shot her a frustrated look but didn't say anything.

'Not this time,' Angela said firmly. 'Natasha's come along in leaps and bounds, and I will not, I repeat *not*, have you destroy the confidence she's slowly building back up by lecturing to her on the few minus points that may be mentioned on Parents' Night. She's been through enough without that.' She straightened her legs and stood up, stretching to relieve the numbness in her feet. She stopped as soon as she saw his brooding eyes fixed on her, and walked towards the door.

'Shall I expect you there tomorrow evening for seven-thirty?' she asked, in a polite voice that still managed to convey total implacability on the subject, and he nodded.

'Do I have a choice?' he asked drily, and she raised her eyebrows.

'None at all.'

Afterwards, in bed, she couldn't quite believe that she had managed to say what she'd had to say with such detached composure. That was precisely how she should be in his presence all the time, and not just when Natasha was the subject of the discussion. Cool, competent, direct, in control. Not behaving like a sixteen-year-old teenager with a bad case of infatuation.

Because, she thought, infatuated I am not. She couldn't account for what had happened the night before, apart from putting it down to temporary insanity, but it couldn't possibly be infatuation. Her ability to feel that way about any man had died a death years ago at the hands of Simon Grey. And further, she thought, there's no point in dwelling on it, because it was simply a blip on the horizon, an isolated incident, some weird transgression that will not happen again.

She grabbed her book and tried to concentrate furiously on what she was reading, but there appeared to be quite a lot of convoluted love affairs, which had the unfortunate result of making her think of Nick, so she abandoned that and switched on the portable television instead. She hardly watched television at all, and late-night viewing, on at least three of the channels, appeared to be given over to yet more subject matter that set her thoughts down unwelcome paths. She settled for political debate on the last channel, and only switched it off when her eyes were too leaden to continue watching. She fell asleep. Promptly and thoughtlessly.

She didn't mention to Natasha the following morning that she had inveigled her uncle into attending the 'Parents' evening. The little bits of cheerfulness which had been popping up now and again over the past few weeks seemed to have crystallised into full-blown good humour, and Natasha was unexpectedly full of an eight-year-old's joy in life. She had read all of her library book, she had worked on some maths which had been giving her problems and had finally reached a satisfying point of comprehension and, after her initial doubts, a delayed sense of happiness at the fact that she wouldn't be sent away to a boarding-school seemed to have filled her overnight.

Angela let herself be carried along on the tide, and was vastly rewarded when Natasha informed her, casually and almost in passing, that she was quite glad that Angela had come to live with them.

She had lived for this day, this one day when she might mean something in her daughter's life. Slowly it was arriving and, although it posed problems of its own, she was happy enough to set them aside—at least for the moment.

Why spoil the mood by introducing Nick's name into the conversation? She knew from experience that Natasha would instantly withdraw into her shell and it would be a case, yet again, of one step forward, two backwards.

At a little after seven she headed for the school, promising Eva that she would be back within an hour and a half, and reassuring Natasha that retribution would not be sought if the reports were less than anticipated.

'Trust me,' she said, taking a big risk and kissing Natasha on the forehead.

Natasha shrugged, but in the dim light of the bedroom she looked gratifyingly pleased, either at the words or the gesture—Angela couldn't be too sure.

'I guess,' she said, which was enough of an affirmative to make Angela smile broadly.

Which she was still doing when she arrived at the school twenty minutes later. Nick was not yet there, but then again she was early. She had no doubt that he would get there. Whatever his faults, and Lord only knew she could think of millions of them offhand, he was a man of his word. It seemed an anomaly, when she sat and thought about it, that she could find him unbearably infuriating, dangerous and far too aware of his own soaring intelligence, yet at the same time utterly trustworthy.

While she waited for him to show up she wandered among the other parents there, relishing the idea that she herself was a parent, even if no one knew. She hated the thought that this was an occasion which should always have been hers, *could* have been hers if only things had been different at the time, if only there had been a way out. She felt a sickening feeling as a rush of imaginary events, lost possibilities, swamped her mind, and she had to switch it off and concentrate on something else.

The school building could not have been more difficult from the one where she had taught. It was old and scrupulously maintained. Artwork by the girls was pinned to a long rectangular noticeboard against one wall, and against another were samples of work—essays—and Angela inspected these minutely.

The headmistress came across to her. She was a small, thin woman in her forties, with a formidable expression, and she seemed to know a great deal about Natasha and her work.

While she chatted Angela listened and kept her eyes open for Nick. When she did see him standing at the door, scouring the room, she felt her heartbeat pick up and she waved across to him.

'I was just telling Miss Field,' the headmistress said, 'about how pleased we are with Natasha's work. I can't say that we weren't a little worried when she first came to us, but things have improved enormously in the past few weeks.'

Angela felt a glowing sense of pride, which she had to stifle under a display of modesty, but as soon as the headmistress had left Nick turned to her and said drily,

'Enough compliments there to last you a lifetime, I should think.'

They strolled across the room to look at the work on the walls, and Angela quenched the strangest feeling of being part of a couple, just a normal couple there to discuss their child's work.

Nothing, of course, could have been further from the truth, but it was as though a door had been opened and she had had a glimpse of something tantalising, some vision of what a relationship could be like.

Wrong scenario, she thought, shaking herself out of her introspection. Wrong man, wrong situation, wrong everything. But for the first time she saw precisely what she had been missing out on all her life, and the vision hurt more than she could ever have dreamed possible.

CHAPTER SIX

THEY drove back in their separate cars. It had been a satisfying meeting. Natasha's work was everything that Angela had predicted. Steadily improving, with none of those worrying signs of one step forward, five steps back, which had been the hallmark of her work ever since she had joined the school earlier on in the year. She was finally beginning to settle down, and there had been, her teacher had assured them, far fewer bursts of rebellious stubborn silence. She had become, in other words, more reachable.

Angela would have liked to think that her contribution might have had something to do with that, but she had to acknowledge that perhaps Natasha had passed through her period of mourning and was emerging on the other side of her own free will. The fact that *I* happen to be on the scene may just be coincidence, Angela told herself. She couldn't afford to let herself imagine for a moment that she had been the turning point, because that would be the first step down the road of thinking that she was becoming indispensable to her daughter, and life had given her enough hard knocks for her to know that optimism could be a dangerous thing.

She manoeuvred her car into the parking slot at the side of the house, and was heading for the door when she heard the crunch of tyres on the drive behind her.

Out of politeness, she waited for Nick to get out of his car.

He had been true to his word. He had listened to what the teacher had to say, his shrewd eyes narrowed, and he had asked courteous, interested questions. He had not flinched when the teacher had described Natasha's poor attitude and even poorer work results of earlier on in the term.

She turned when she heard his car door slam, and was already heading up to the front door when she felt his hand on her arm. She pulled back, an automatic gesture which didn't go unnoticed, because he dropped her arm and stepped back slightly.

'Congratulations,' he said in a deceptively mild voice. 'You were in such a rush to leave after the meeting that I don't think I had a chance to say that.'

'Thank you.' She could feel herself reluctantly frozen to the spot. The darkness masked the hard lines of his face, but she could feel him staring at her intently nevertheless.

'How about a spot of dinner?' he asked.

It was a request that seemed to have been issued so startlingly out of the blue that she looked at him mutely and then repeated, parrot-style, 'Dinner?'

'To discuss what was said with Mrs Pritchard. We're two civilised human beings—we can round the evening off interacting in a pleasant, mature manner, don't you think? Besides, I want to discuss your contract with you, and now's as good a time as any.'

'What do you want to discuss about my contract?' Angela asked, suddenly wary.

'I'll go and ask Eva whether she can babysit for a couple more hours. My car's open. Why don't you let yourself in? Warmer than standing outside.'

He strode towards the front door and vanished inside the house, leaving Angela feeling slightly battered, as though she had been run over by a steamroller which she hadn't even seen coming.

Very slowly she made her way to his car and slid into the passenger seat. Then she crossed her legs and primly waited until he reappeared a few minutes later, a shadowy outline with his back to the fully lit hallway behind him, growing more distinct as he walked briskly towards the car and then slipped into the driver's seat and started the engine.

'Now,' he said, turning to face her, 'where would you like to eat?'

'I don't care,' Angela said. 'Somewhere quick,' she added without thinking, and he eyed her narrowly.

'You have a talent,' he grated, reversing and then slowly edging down the drive to the main road, 'for making the most innocuous of comments sound remarkably like insults.'

'I'm sorry,' she said, face averted. She preferred to know that he misunderstood her shortness as rudeness rather than saw the truth—which was that he made her feel nervous, and nerves made her jumpy and abrupt in his presence.

She hoped that wherever he chose to eat would be somewhere in the fast food line, but it was a slim chance. She doubted that Nick Cameron ever stepped inside a fast food place if he could help it, and she wasn't surprised when, after a drive in almost complete silence, they pulled up outside a small Italian restaurant with the sort of expensive cars outside that predicted a bijou menu with astronomical prices.

She wasn't disappointed. The head waiter showed them to a table, one of only two still unoccupied, with the sort of smiling subservience which Nick accepted virtually as his due.

He also appeared to be known there, because as soon as they were seated out wafted a tall, well-groomed man—the owner, it transpired—who made jovial conversation with him for a few minutes and tentatively tried to arrange a game of squash, to which suggestion Nick replied that only his secretary could fix dates like that.

'My life is not my own,' Nick said ruefully. 'I virtually have to consult my office diary to find out whether I can have a bath!'

'Good to see that you still find the time to wine and dine a charming female, however,' the man, introduced as Alistair, said. He turned to Angela and flashed her a smile which coming from anyone else would have seemed slightly offensive and patronising, but it was so in character with the rest of him that she found herself smiling back.

'I'm afraid you've misread the situation,' she corrected him, amused but anxious to dispel any picture he might have of her as Nick Cameron's lucky dinner companion. 'I work for Mr Cameron. I look after his niece. In fact we've just come back from a parent-teacher evening.'

Alistair's eyebrows shot up. 'You managed to drag him away from making millions for *that*?'

'These things are very important,' Angela said, laughing. 'I'm afraid I was forced to leave him no option.'

At which Alistair flashed them a brief, thoughtful glance before bustling off to his 'bubbling cauldrons', as he put it, and Nick turned to her with a look of amusement.

'I think I should point out that you've just shot my reputation down in flames,' he said, picking up the menu and scanning it very quickly. He looked at her, and continued looking at her even while he beckoned the wine waiter across to the table and ordered a bottle of Italian white wine.

'What are you talking about?'

'Put it this way: Alistair Davies will be chuckling over the image of me being dictated to by a woman for the next few months.'

Angela looked at him with some surprise. 'You prefer the role of "Me Tarzan, you Jane", do you? I thought that that sort of thing had died a death in the Middle Ages.'

Nick leaned back in his chair and surveyed her with such inscrutability that she began to feel a little disconcerted. 'You'd be amazed at how many women still like men to make the decisions.'

'Disappointed might be a better word,' she said, and he laughed, a low-throated laugh that contained enough pleasure to disconcert her even more.

'You don't approve?'

I thought we were here to discuss what Mrs Pritchard had said and to talk about my contract, she felt like pointing out. How was it that he always managed to manoeuvre the conversation to suit himself?

'What's the point of a woman, or anyone for that matter, having a mind if she doesn't bother to exert it?' She fiddled with her wine glass and then made a game attempt to drag the conversation to where it originally should have been. 'These meetings with teachers are important. Mrs Pritchard sees Natasha, during term-time, at least as much as we do, if not a lot more. If we want any questions answered about how she's doing, intellectually as well as emotionally, then she's the person who can answer them.' She paused. 'Are you listening to me?'

'Yes, ma'am.'

Angela frowned. Was he having a quick laugh at her expense? Difficult to tell, precisely, when the only lighting came from an assortment of candles on tables and some very subdued overhead bulbs.

The waiter sidled up with their starters, then sidled away again, and in between mouthfuls Nick remarked, with some satisfaction, that he was delighted with the reports on his niece. 'You must be very pleased yourself,' he commented, closing his knife and fork and relaxing back.

'Yes, I am. Very.'

'Of course, with your past experience you must have felt that thrill of success before? At seeing a difficult child begin to succeed?'

'I suppose so,' she murmured without looking up. 'But this is different.'

'Is it? Why?' His voice was soft and low, but that didn't stop the sudden clamour of alarm bells in her head.

'Because...' she said with a vague smile. 'Because, I guess, of the personal link I have with her. Through your sister.'

She wondered whether to involve herself in this explanation a bit more and decided against it. She could easily find herself becoming entangled. So far, things had been moving smoothly. Far more smoothly than she could ever have expected when she had sent that desperate letter to him in America all that time ago. It would be too easy to let complacency slip in—and complacency could end up costing her dearly.

'Also...' she continued briskly, pushing away the plate in front of her and linking her fingers on the table. She assumed an earnest expression. 'Also...this is really the first time that I've ever worked with a child on a totally one-to-one basis. It's quite different from dealing with a classroom full of children, all clamouring for their share of attention.'

'And just as rewarding?'

'Yes, I think so.' Far, far more rewarding, she thought. A million times more so. In fact, comparisons don't really exist.

'Which brings me to the subject of your contract,' Nick said smoothly, as dishes were cleared away and various new articles of cutlery carefully replaced the used ones.

Angela felt a chill run down her spine, even though she was sensible enough to know, logically, that he would hardly be considering dismissing her when he had already expressed satisfaction with Natasha and so, implicitly, with her.

But so much hinged on him. To think about it was to be overwhelmed, and there was a constant, nagging fear that he might see right through the truth, the half-truths and the downright fabrications to the real reasons that she was so desperate to keep this job. Deception was not something he would forgive easily, and there was a very real possibility that if he ever found out her true identity he might send her packing, on the grounds that she might prove ultimately destructive to Natasha's security. Wasn't it, after all, left to the child to find her parent and not the other way around in situations such as this?

She smiled and hustled the thought away.

'Yes. My contract.'

'Originally I told you that you would be working for me on a probationary period. Well, already I've seen the changes you've made to Natasha...'

'She made them herself. I just helped.'

'However you care to put it is fine with me. The fact is that, however sceptical I was of you to start with, you're doing a good job—which is why I'm going to offer you an increase in the salary we originally agreed on.' He named the increase and she very nearly choked on her wine.

She hadn't been expecting this. She watched him in a slightly gaping fashion, and then said, 'Why? Why would you want to do that?'

Food appeared in front of them, served with aplomb. Sole for both of them, off the bone and looking ridiculously huge on their plates. Angela used the opportunity to look down so that she could get her thoughts back together.

'Have you ever heard about the financial trap?' Nick asked conversationally, tucking into his food with gusto. Where on earth did he put it? she wondered. Did he have the sort of body that metamorphosed calories into muscle?

'It's what happens to people who find themselves in a job where they're paid so much that they're extremely reluctant to leave and look elsewhere for something else. I suppose you could say that it's a way for an employer to buy a certain amount of loyalty from his employees.' He sipped a mouthful of wine and looked at her over the rim of his glass.

'You can't buy people,' she said automatically, and he smiled at her slowly and cynically.

'You've led an extremely sheltered life if you believe that.'

'Are you telling me that you're buying my loyalty?'

'That's right.' He said it as though it was the most natural thing in the world. 'As I said to you from the very beginning, Natasha needs stability—and I intend to pay you enough to ensure that stability is precisely what she gets.'

'There's no need,' Angela objected. In fact, little did

he know, but there was no need to pay her anything at all to get the devotion required. She had enough of it to last a lifetime.

'Tell me what you're running away from and I'll tell you whether there's a need or not.'

'I've told you already—I'm not running away from anything.'

'In that case, you can look on it as a bonus of sorts.'

'Thank you very much,' she replied. She continued eating, contemplating the irony of his offer and what had motivated it, and after a while she said curiously, 'Do you always operate this way?'

'What way?'

'Do you always feel that you can buy people?'

He shrugged. 'I assume that you consider that a very cynical outlook on life?'

'Don't *you*?'

'It's a cruel world out there, and it's as well to look reality full in the face instead of hiding behind rose-tinted spectacles. I'm not saying that everyone has their price. By no means. Nor am I saying that money will buy you everything you want. It's simply something that oils the wheels of day to day living.'

'Oh,' she said, for want of anything better. 'Maybe I *have* led a sheltered life in that case.'

'You're not completely ingenuous, though, are you? There's a core of steel somewhere inside you. Now, where do you think that came from?'

'I don't know what you're talking about.' She closed her knife and fork and looked at her watch in a fairly pointed manner. 'Is it all right if we skip coffee? I've got to be up early tomorrow. Natasha has her swimming class before school beings.' She gave him a bright, polite smile and he smiled back at her, but somehow the smile didn't quite reach his eyes. No, his eyes remained thoughtful, calculating.

But he conceded without argument, and on the drive back indulged in the sort of light conversation that made it easy for her to relax.

In the morning, she would tell Natasha how well the parents' evening had gone. She looked through the window and imagined the smile on her daughter's face, that shy, defensive, childlike smile that could turn a cloudy day into a sunny one.

She allowed herself the luxury of imagining years of cultivating that smile, until it became natural and automatic, until all the shadows were dispelled for both of them. In her mind she saw Natasha two years hence, then five years hence, on the threshold of womanhood, then down through the years, and for once she didn't pull herself up and deliver an internal lecture on the stupidity of imagining anything in a future that was still so very uncertain.

It came as almost a surprise when she realised that they were back at the house, and that the atmosphere between them was relaxed enough to be almost convivial.

And a peculiar thought struck her as, later, she got ready for bed.

Nick Cameron was perhaps the only person in the world to whom she would ever want to confess what was really going on in her head. It was such an odd notion that she actually shook her head to clear the thought away. Except the thought didn't disappear at all. It simply resettled into a slightly different shape.

By the following morning, she had forgotten that it had ever existed. She was so full of the pleasure of telling Natasha how the evening with her teacher had gone, so thrilled to see that fleeting smile.

'I'm so proud of you,' she said on the spur of the moment, and she wasn't even deflated when Natasha asked why.

'Because...because I just am.' She began feeling sentimental and tearful, and said in a more cheerful, down-to-earth voice that the portrait which she had been painting was nearly finished, that only a few more sittings were required and that she was planning on doing a still life next. It was amazing the emotions that could be hidden successfully underneath babble.

She really was planning on doing a still life. As soon as she got back to the house after taking Natasha to school, she decided to get on with it, and was carefully arranging a dispirited assortment of fruit around the base of a desk lamp when the doorbell rang. She heard it very dimly in the background and chose to ignore it, since Eva was bustling downstairs somewhere and would get it.

Whoever it was, it wouldn't be for her. She had kept in touch with her friends, and, more to avoid Nick's easily aroused curiosity than anything else, had in fact spent one weekend back in the village—looking up old faces, making animated conversation and secretly longing for Sunday to arrive so that she could rush back down to London.

When asked where she was living, she had distributed vague answers, even though none of her ex-colleagues knew anything about her past and could hardly be a danger. Why risk anything? Nick might have given her a pay rise and informed her that he wanted her to stay, but he still harboured suspicions—he was still prowling, looking for the secret he was convinced she was hiding.

She sighed and was sceptically eyeing the display of fruit, which was doing a good job of sabotaging her artistic instinct, when she heard a knock on the door and Eva peered round and informed her that she had a visitor.

'Who is it?' she asked, surprised and instantly cautious, to which Eva unhelpfully replied that she had put her in the sitting room. Angela had the amusing image of someone being bodily deposited onto one of the flowered chairs, like a sack of potatoes.

She was still grinning to herself when she pushed open the door and discovered, with dismay, that her guest was the last person she wanted to see: Philippa Ames, standing with her back to the door, looking out into the garden.

Her posture was perfectly straight, like a mannequin dressed in an expensive designer suit, one hand on her waist, the other at her side.

Oh, good grief, Angela thought, stepping into the room and closing the door behind her. The High Priestess of Nightmares has arrived.

'Eva told me that you wanted to see me,' she said, edging towards a chair like someone trying to avoid invisible laser beams.

Philippa turned around slowly. 'I hope I'm not disturbing you.'

'I was about to do some painting.' She thought about the uninspiring fruit and grimaced. 'Would you like something to drink? Tea? Coffee?' Special brew of bats' wings and eyes of newt?

'No, thank you.' She swayed towards a chair, sat down gracefully and crossed her legs. 'I won't be long. Mustn't keep you from a work of art, must I? I just came for a little chat.'

That was ominous enough to have Angela wishing for a very stiff drink.

'I phoned last night to speak to Nick, and Eva informed me that you and he had gone to dinner.'

'Ye-e-es...'

'I had no idea that you two were so close.' Philippa
tilted her head to one side, so that the observation turned
into a question.

So this is what the visit is all about, Angela thought
indignantly. More veiled threats to keep away from her
dearly beloved. She tried to keep as exquisitely still as
Philippa, but her body refused to obey. She found herself
fidgeting, tucking her hair behind her ears.

'We're not *close*, Philippa,' she said wearily, 'and I
should have thought that a busy career woman like yourself would have had better things to do than come here
to have this conversation with me. If you must know,
Nick and I went to Natasha's Parents' Evening and he
thought that it would be a nice idea to have a meal out
afterwards and discuss what her teacher had said.'

'Very cosy,' Philippa said acidly. 'Wouldn't it have
been more in keeping to have come back here and discussed whatever needed to be discussed over a cup of
coffee? Employer/employee style?'

Angela could feel two spots of colour burning her
cheeks, marks of anger which Philippa obviously mistook
for guilt, because her glacial green eyes narrowed and
her fingers clenched onto her knee. Long fingers, with
pearly pink manicured nails.

'If you feel that way, why on earth don't you ask Nick
instead of me?'

'Men are usually blind to what's happening under their
own noses. They can be as sharp as knives when it comes
to working their way through the concrete jungle, they
can be clever at financial analysis and they can run multi-
national companies with one hand tied behind their back,
but that doesn't make them astute when it comes to fig-
uring out what's going on in a woman's head.'

'I wouldn't know about that. Look, I really think that this conversation—'

'It seems that Nick can't see what's been perfectly obvious to me from day one.'

'Which is…?'

'Which is that there's more to you than meets the eyes. A hell of a lot more. And do you know something? I don't trust women who have something to hide.'

Angela didn't say anything. Firstly, there was nothing *to* say, as far as she was concerned, and secondly, she was becoming used to accusations of hiding things.

'Why are you here, Miss Field? Really?'

'I'm here to help look after Natasha,' she explained patiently, using the long-suffering voice of someone who was being compelled to explain something very simple over and over again. 'I knew Nick's sister and I thought that it would be a nice idea if… Well, I honestly don't think that I have to justify my presence here to you, Miss Ames. I'm here, I'm doing a good job, Nick is perfectly happy with my work and I really must ask you not to keep coming here and grilling me.'

'In other words, leave you a clear field.' Philippa was sitting forward in the chair now, and her face was as white and as cold as marble.

'In other words, let me get on with doing the job that I'm being paid to do.'

'Did you know that Nick and I used to be lovers?' Philippa relaxed back, recrossed her long legs and watched Angela with the intentness of a snake eyeing its next meal.

Used to be? Angela felt her heart give a little leap and she stifled the feeling.

'Yes. I might as well be honest with you because I want you to know exactly where you stand and exactly where I stand. We were very…involved with one another when he lived in New York. He's a powerful man, hard to resist and wealthy as well. In other words, a very big fish. There were a lot of women out there who would have loved nothing better than to get their claws into him.'

Philippa linked her fingers together on her lap. Cold, straightforward, laying her cards on the table. 'It ended because business and pleasure, in the end, don't seem to mix very well. I'm telling you all this so that you know how things stand, so that you know that whatever little schemes you have lined up your sleeve I am a threat that has no intention of going away.'

'I don't care one way or another whether you stay or leave, and I don't particularly like being threatened.'

Philippa ignored this. 'Nick was attracted to me in the past. I intend to remind him that he still is. I intend to marry him, and when I do the first person I shall get rid of is you. After that I shall send Natasha to a boarding-school, which is where she belongs. Do you understand me?'

'I understand that you have wasted your time coming here, Miss Ames.' Angela stood up stiffly and walked towards the door. 'I would appreciate it if you would leave now.' She opened the door and waited, watching as Philippa unhurriedly walked towards her, completely relaxed, the competitor assured of victory. There was even a small smile playing at the corners of her mouth.

'I hope you remember our little conversation,' she said, stopping to look at Angela, 'and get any silly notions you may have out of your head.'

Angela didn't say anything. She had never encountered such overt hostility before and it sapped her defences. Was this really how people operated? Was Philippa just more open about it? Were relationships more about ownership than about love? Perhaps she was the abnormal one, she thought. Perhaps she had held herself so far back from the field of play that she no longer understood the rules. Or maybe the rich simply had rules of their own.

She couldn't believe that someone as shrewd as Nick couldn't see through someone as obviously manipulative as Philippa, but then Philippa had a point. Men, from everything she had read and seen from the sidelines, could be peculiarly blind when it came to women. They could be swept off their feet by a show of flamboyance, a tantalising hint of promise, a waft of perfume, only to find themselves in a trap of their own making.

And, after all, Nick *had* gone out with Philippa. Slept with her. She had no reason to doubt that. And if it had happened once, what was to say that it wouldn't happen again?

She headed back to her studio and tried to get down her canvas and her paints, but her hands wouldn't do her bidding. Philippa's visit had set her mind whirring on a course that left no room for anything but thoughts—confused, disturbing thoughts.

She hated the idea of them together. Philippa and Nick. Nick and Philippa. A twosome. Sharing meals, sharing conversation, sharing a bed. When she thought about that she could feel her body go limp, as though her bones had suddenly turned to sponge.

I'm *jealous*! she thought. It was a sensation that she had not felt before. She had simply never let herself get close enough to anyone actually to feel jealous of them.

Even Simon, she thought, had never inspired the kind of savage emotion that was tearing away inside her now. She had been swept off her feet then, and so young— young enough to think that the world was at her command. Her feelings had not been fully formed then. But they must be now, because when she sat back in her chair and thought of those long white arms wrapped around Nick's body she had to close her eyes to try and clear the image.

After a while—she didn't know how long—she heard Eva bustling outside in the corridor, and when she looked at her watch she found that she had spent nearly two hours in the room, staring at the canvas while time ticked by. Valuable time.

Without really thinking, and mostly because she no longer had any desire to be indoors—and never mind the sad collection of fruit which sat there, reminding her of her urge to paint—she left the house and went into the West End. And shopped.

It was an activity in which she rarely indulged, but then, when she had been teaching she had had to think carefully about her money. Now, and especially with the increase in her salary to come, money was no longer the problem it had used to be. In fact, she was saving on a fairly spectacular scale.

She bought a dress—slim-fitting with polka dots, very short. She bought shoes—high black ones, which seemed wicked and enticing compared with her array of comfortable footwear back at the house. She bought some skirts, also short, and a pair of silk trousers which felt like cool water against her skin.

She also bought Natasha a hat. A blue denim, floppy hat, turned up at the front and pinned back with a little spray of silk flowers. That lifted her spirits—much more, in fact, than her purchases for herself had done.

'You look miserable,' Natasha said as soon as she climbed into the car that afternoon. She was all blithe candour, which, rather than making Angela even more aware of her frame of mind, made her grin.

'I was. So I went shopping,' she said, which made Natasha's eyes pop open, as though shopping was an unheard of exercise, at least as far as Angela was concerned. 'A few clothes,' Angela went on loftily. 'And I bought you something as well.'

As soon as they arrived home the hat was duly tried on, amidst a great deal of blushing on Natasha's part. And Angela got a hug—a quick one, but still, it felt to Angela as though she had suddenly won the National Lottery.

But as soon as Natasha was in bed, and the silence of the house had settled around her, she began to feel anxiety and worry gnaw away at her again.

Philippa, Philippa, Philippa. Despite all her brave words it all came down to Philippa and her warnings.

I can't afford to leave this part of my life behind, she thought. I've paid for my mistakes and I'm just not going to start paying again. She tried to contemplate a life without Natasha in it, and a core of steely resolve hardened inside her.

She attempted to think logically, to tell herself that Nick was his own master and, despite what Philippa had said, he was not susceptible to female wiles. And she might have believed it if she hadn't seen the determination on that beautiful, faultless face.

What man, she thought miserably, could resist someone like Philippa? She had a model's looks and self-confidence, and a clever brain as well, just to make matters worse.

If she got what she so badly wanted, which was Nick, she would see to it that Angela became the first casualty. Which means, Angela thought, that she mustn't get him. I can trust my basic instincts, which tell me that he's perceptive enough to see through Philippa's manoeuvrings, but then again, my instincts may be way off target. And there is so much at stake.

Since when, she thought reasonably enough, am I some kind of a guru when it comes to understanding what motivates a man? Philippa is probably three million times more experienced than I am.

In fact, she concluded, I misread the only man I ever really went out with so comprehensively that I am the last candidate eligible to win the 'guess what motivates a man' competition.

So what do I do?

But she knew even as she asked herself the question. Maybe, subconsciously, she had known the minute she had left the house and gone out shopping. She thought of the polka-dot dress hanging pristine in her wardrobe, and the high black shoes with their devil-may-care allure.

My answer, she decided, lies there.

CHAPTER SEVEN

STEP one, she decided, was to stop avoiding him. Even she knew that the art of seduction did not involve treating the seduced-to-be as though he were an infectious disease.

That evening she made herself stay in the sitting room far longer than she usually did, waiting for Nick to arrive back.

It all seemed like a cold-blooded game, but what else, she asked herself over and over again, could she do? She certainly couldn't just sit back and allow Philippa to dazzle him with her glamour and her intelligence until he became a sitting target for whatever she had in mind.

Not that it helped. The minute he walked into the room, tugging at his tie to loosen the top button of his shirt, she felt her stomach clench and unclench, and it took a lot of will-power not to spring to her feet and head for the door.

Instead, she made herself stay right where she was. She even made herself say in a perfectly normal voice, 'Hello. How was your day?'

Nick stopped in his tracks and looked at her with his eyebrows raised. 'What are you doing still up? I thought that nine-thirty was your bedtime?'

'I wasn't tired, so I decided to stay down here and...'

'Wait for me to arrive so that you could ask me about my day...?'

This was said with such disbelief that for a minute she was tempted to abandon her ridiculous plan and leave.

'Or is there some other pressing concern you want to talk to me about? Don't tell me that Natasha is acting up again?'

He removed his jacket, tossed it onto one of the chairs and began rolling up the sleeves of his shirt. Angela followed the movements with her eyes as surreptitiously as she could, and felt her face begin to go hot.

Not exactly a cold-blooded game, she thought fleetingly. Why deny the truth? I'm attracted to him. Except she wasn't sure whether this made things easier or more difficult. What if, after all her efforts, he rejected her? She tried not to start down the path of making comparisons between herself and Philippa, and instead smiled what she hoped was a carefree smile.

'Oh, no, nothing like that. Natasha's fine. She's getting through her homework faster and faster these days. She's really rather bright, as a matter of fact. Way above average.' She felt a swell of pride at the thought.

'Good. I'm pleased to hear it.' He went across to the bar, and asked over his shoulder whether she wanted a drink.

'Yes!' she almost shouted, then quickly modulated the tone of her voice. 'Yes, please, that would be very nice.'

'What would you like?'

At this juncture, she thought, I should deepen my voice to a throaty purr, say something suggestive along the lines of Tell me what you've got, and then opt for a Scotch on the rocks.

That seemed to be at a rather more advanced stage of the seduction game, though, so she dithered indecisively, frowning, until he said, at last, 'It's not a world-shattering decision. How about a gin and tonic?'

'Gin and tonic. Yes! That would be great.'

She was wearing one of her new purchases. A short cream-coloured skirt, which wrapped around and buttoned at the side, and a body-hugging sleeveless top in dark green. She recrossed her legs and wondered whether it was her imagination or whether most of them were exposed in this position.

When he handed her the glass she saw his eyes sweep over her body, vaguely bemused.

'Now.' He sat down next to her on the sofa, with one arm stretched along the back, and turned to her. 'What can I do for you?'

My reply at this point, she thought, should be, Now there's a question! What would you like to do…?

'I was bored,' she answered, taking a very small sip of her drink and not caring for it. 'I fancied a chat. I guess when you asked about whether my one-to-one relationship with Natasha was as rewarding as teaching a classroom of children I was being perfectly honest when I said yes. But I do sometimes miss the interaction of adult company.' That was true enough to make her sound slightly apologetic, and he threw her a wry smile.

'I can understand that. I personally can't think of anything worse than being cooped up on my own, without anyone around, for an indefinite period of time.'

'I take it you've never had any serious illnesses, then?' She relaxed and decided that she would manoeuvre herself into seduction mode a little later. After she had finished her drink. Right now, it just seemed easier to let the flow of their conversation take its course.

'Absolutely none, Doctor.' He laughed and raked his fingers through his hair, then continued to look at her quizzically.

Angela took another sip of gin and tonic and found it

slightly more bearable this time. 'You never told me how your day was.'

'Would you care to tell me what's going on?' he asked lazily, putting his drink on the table at the side of him and focusing his full attention on her.

'Nothing's going on! You're the one who said that we were two civilised human beings who could interact in a mature way, so here I am. Interacting.'

'And you're the one who said that we need never meet except in passing—which, incidentally, you have made a point of doing ever since you arrived here.'

Angela shrugged and looked at him in a distracted way. She would have to do better than this, she thought. She would at least have to rustle up some amusing conversation from up her sleeve if she were to sustain his interest, never mind arouse his male approval.

'I changed my mind.'

'Woman's prerogative?'

'Something like that.'

'And here I was thinking that you were individual enough not to fall back on stereotyped excuses like that.' His eyes were amused but shuttered. 'My day, since you seem so interested, has seen me running from one meeting to another without enough time in between to catch my breath.'

'Sounds awful,' Angela said truthfully.

'I expect it does,' he agreed politely. 'And what about yours? Riddled with excitement?'

This, she reflected miserably, wasn't going at all well. He might have suffered a brief, lapse of sanity that one time he had made a pass at her, but clearly he was well over that, and now she was beginning to feel a fool.

'I made an effort to do some painting—a still life of some fruit—but I couldn't get down to it so I went shopping instead.' She swallowed quite a substantial amount of her drink and her face went even hotter. She very nearly spluttered, in fact.

'Why is it that women always seem to go shopping when they can't get down to anything else?'

'Why is it,' Angela answered, forgetting her nerves for a minute, 'that men make such sweeping statements in such patronising voices?'

He laughed, and this time when he looked at her there was appreciation in his grey eyes.

'As a matter of fact,' she continued, 'I almost never go shopping. Not unless I have to. Shopping is a habit, and I've never got into that particular habit.'

'How is that?' He folded his arms and appeared to be enjoying the conversation, in that slightly amused, slightly cynical way of his. Either that or his mind was a million miles away and he was adopting this attentive, interested air only because it was second nature to him.

'Never had the money, I suppose.'

'Not even pocket money as a teenager? Carefully saved up and spent on make-up to be worn only when your parents weren't looking?'

'Maybe that's how it works in some families, but not in mine.' She thought of her fractured family life, and heard herself saying, 'There was no money floating about in our house. No mother, in fact. Just a father, who had a bit of a drinking problem.' The confession, once out, horrified her. Say something! she thought, because he was just sitting there, watching her in silence.

Eventually he took the empty glass from her, refilled it without asking, and said, as he handed it to her, 'You're very brave. To have pulled yourself up and got where you have. It must have been hard.'

The genuine sympathy in his voice filled her with an unexpected dose of self-pity, and she gave a small laugh.

'I never really considered that at the time. I just lived on a day-to-day basis, working at doing something with my life. Very dull, I'm afraid. No wild parties, no bars, no clubs. Just books.' She felt so self-conscious that she would have launched into a monologue on weather patterns just to change the subject. She couldn't remember the last time she had been tempted to confide in anyone. She didn't think that she ever had, come to think of it.

'Natasha's a very lucky little girl,' she carried on in a rush. 'You were right when you said that money doesn't buy everything, but it certainly helps to reduce some of the struggle.'

I'm boring him, she thought. He doesn't look bored, but he must be—sitting here at the end of a long, tiring day, listening to my dreary problems.

'She'll have her fair share of problems when she gets older, don't you think?'

Angela racked her brain. He sounded as though she should have inside knowledge of what would be afflicting Natasha in the years to come, but for the life of her she hadn't a clue what he was talking about. So she guessed.

'Of course it'll be hard,' she said, 'with your sister and her husband not around.'

'My sister and her husband...' He looked at her carefully. 'Why do you always refer to Natasha's parents as "my sister and her husband"? I don't think that I have ever heard you refer to them as her mother and father, or even as her parents.'

'Haven't you?' She was beginning to regret her grand plan to seduce Nick Cameron. He had a relentlessly suspicious mind, and, aside from the fact that she would be doing something which went against her nature, there was a higher than fifty percent chance that he wouldn't be taken in for an instant. If, that was, he was attracted to her at all.

When it comes right down to it, she thought to herself, I just haven't got the nerve, or the cool to go through with it. Not to mention the glamour. She thought of Natasha, and of what would happen if Philippa had her way, and clenched her fists together in an agony of indecision.

'No. You haven't.'

Angela shrugged. 'You must have a memory like a computer bank if you remember every word I've ever said.'

'Not every word.'

But just about, his voice implied, and she tried not to look too alarmed.

'What problems do *you* think Natasha will have to face?' she asked bluntly.

'Adopted children have more than their fare share of potential problems, don't you think?'

'Yes, I suppose they do.'

But I'm her mother, and I'm here, she thought, and she won't have those problems because everything will come right in the end. She had to live on some hope. Too much reality, she had realised early on, could become a crippling handicap. It could stop you putting one foot in front of the other.

'I expect, in due course, she will want to find out the identity of her real mother.'

'I expect so.' She felt as though she was treading on thin ice.

'Traumatic enough if Clive and Amanda had been alive. Worse now, in Natasha's case.' He leaned forward with his elbows on his knees, and it was all she could do not to automatically edge back into her chair.

'I expect so,' she said again.

'You seem very monosyllabic on the subject. Suddenly exhausted after your brief burst of conversation with me?'

'No, of course not,' Angela said, wondering how her plans had gone so badly wrong.

'Tell me, have you had any experience with adopted children? Have you taught any? Have you ever had any personal encounter with the problems that can arise?'

'No! Natasha's still a child! Isn't it better to face those problems as and when they arise?'

Nick stood up and stretched, and stuck his hands in his pockets. 'You could be right.' He was beginning to sound faintly bored with the subject. 'I think I'll head up. Are you going to remain down here?' He moved towards the door and threw an enquiring glance in her direction. She hastily got to her feet.

At this point in her calculations, if all had gone perfectly according to plan, he should have been looking at her with thinly veiled desire, and even if they had both gone to their separate bedrooms the image of Philippa would have been banished from his mind for good. And that, she reflected, had been naïvety bordering on sheer stupidity.

She brushed past him, and as she headed up the stairs he said, from behind her, 'Natasha's biggest problem, of course, will be when she discovers that her mother is at best a disappointment, and at worst a nightmare.'

'Why should she be either of those two?' Angela asked in a controlled voice. She turned on the staircase to look at him, for once on his eye level.

'It follows, doesn't it? What sort of woman abandons

her baby at birth? Hardly someone with a strong nurturing instinct.'

It felt as though he had slapped her on the face. A deep feeling of despair and sadness and anger formed like a ball inside her stomach. If she reached down she would be able to feel it, throbbing against the palm of her hand.

'Another sweeping generalisation?' she asked with cold contempt. 'Please tell me what gives you the right to make statements like that. I should love to hear. You've had a lot of dealings with women who have abandoned their babies at birth, have you? In your daily line of work?'

'Don't you dare use that tone with me,' he grated.

Angela ignored him. That ball inside her was growing. In a minute, it would explode.

'It may not have occurred to you that there are women who have no option but to do what they do. That at the time it seems the only course open to them. That they live to regret their decision with every passing day.'

He was looking at her very carefully and she modulated her voice. 'I think that what you said was unfair,' she continued in a low voice, much calmer now. Fear at how close she had stepped to the edge gave her a sudden burst of rigid self-control. 'I'm afraid that in teaching I have come across too many unfair things to allow statements like that to go unnoticed. I apologise if I sounded rude.'

'Apology accepted,' he muttered tersely.

She turned away, willing to leave it at that—in fact, desperate to leave it at that—and headed back up the stairs at a run. Her feet were moving but her mind was raging with incoherent, fevered thoughts that made the hairs on her arms stand on end.

She was very nearly at the top when she missed her

footing and stumbled. It was an ungraceful manoeuvre which she was about to correct by standing back upright when she felt his arms move around her and he lifted her up.

The effect on her was similar to running a very high temperature in the space of about four seconds. Her body felt as though it was on fire, and when she opened her mouth to tell him that there was no need to take her to her bedroom, that she was fully capable of walking on her own, a strangled sound emerged that bore no resemblance to her voice.

He kicked open the door with his foot and managed to find his way to the bed in complete darkness. Once he had deposited her on it, he switched on the bedside lamp and sat down next to her.

Was this the intimacy that she had sought in her mind only hours earlier? Odd, but the image she had had of herself in such a situation had been of someone quite controlled, huskily seductive. Certainly not of someone with a burning face and trembling hands.

'Now,' he said, 'let's have a look.' He removed her shoe and ran his fingers expertly over her ankle. Long, cool fingers that sent tiny shivers running through her.

She wanted to draw her foot up to her chest, but her body remained as still as a statue.

'Does it hurt?' he asked, glancing up at her. The shadows thrown by the light made patterns on his face. When he moved, the patterns dispersed and reformed. She could have watched it for ever. Instead she lowered her eyes, and noticed that her very brief skirt appeared even briefer now that she was in a supine position.

'No,' she said, embarrassed. She made a circle with her foot, winced, and said, 'Ouch!'

'I'll get you a couple of painkillers.'

'No, really,' she protested, going redder at this level of fuss. 'There's no need. A good sleep will take care of it, and anyway, I hate taking tablets.'

'A couple of painkillers won't turn you into an addict,' he said drily, standing up. 'I'll be back in a minute.'

Which at least gave her time to reposition her skirt. Whatever happened to seduction? she thought with resignation. Whatever was the point of all these coolly formulated plans if she bolted at the first fence? How was she going to hold onto her daughter if she allowed Philippa to step right in where she wanted to? The questions turned round and round in her head, and she realised that she had answered none of them by the time Nick returned to the room with a glass of water and two capsules, which he held out to her on the palm of his hand.

She swallowed the tablets and thanked him in a demure voice. She expected him to leave, but he didn't.

'Let's have a look and see if you can manage to walk,' he said.

'Of course I can walk,' Angela told him. But she didn't move, because her ankle was throbbing rather more than she had anticipated and she couldn't be bothered to test it to see whether it would stand her weight. 'I've just twisted my ankle! Not broken both legs in a skiing accident!'

He grinned at her and motioned to her to stand up, so she reluctantly moved her legs to the side of the bed, lowered them to the floor then promptly moved them back.

'OK,' she conceded. 'I'd be able to manage a hobble but walking a marathon might be a bit trickier. I'll be fine once these painkillers start to take effect.'

'Where's your nightdress?'

'My what...?'

'Whatever you sleep in.' He stood up and walked across to the chest of drawers, and pulled open the top one.

She couldn't afford for him to begin rummaging through her clothes, so she said sharply, 'Right-hand drawer!'

'Where?' he asked, with his back to her. 'What does it look like?'

'It's a baggy T-shirt with "Keep our green country green" written on it.' She could hear her voice showing signs of becoming sulky, but really this was all very embarrassing. Tripping on a staircase, being levered up and deposited on her bed like a bundle of used laundry, then bossed about like a child.

'This?' He held up the T-shirt between two of his fingers and twirled it around with fascinated curiosity.

'What's wrong with it?' If only her feet had been working she would have leapt from the bed and snatched it out of his hands. As it was, all she could do was content herself with a glare, the ferocity of which was lost in the semi-darkness of the bedroom.

'Unusual garment to sleep in,' was all he said, amused.

'It happens to be very comfortable. You have no idea how impractical those lacy negligée things are.'

'No, I don't suppose I do, having never worn one.' He grinned and strolled back to her slowly, holding out the T-shirt.

'Shall I help you get undressed?'

Angela groaned. 'No, I can manage,' she said, yanking the T-shirt from him before he could reanalyse it and come up with a few more scathing remarks.

Clearly the women he had slept with had never seen comfort as a prime concern when it came to choosing their sleepwear. Had he been fed on a diet of black silk and lace? The sort of stuff worn so that it could later be ripped off in a frenzy of passion? A frenzy of passion was certainly the last thing he was feeling right now, judging from the leftover grin on his face.

'OK. Goodnight.' He let himself out of the bedroom and closed the door behind him, though not completely, leaving a crack of light slithering through.

When she was sure that he had vanished she tried to get off the bed, but was driven back by the stab of pain in her ankle. Nothing hugely dramatic, but uncomfortable enough to ensure that she didn't make standing up a priority. At least not on both legs.

So she unbuttoned her skirt, lying down, wriggled out of it, kicked it off the bed, then eyed the offending ankle malevolently.

Instead of tackling her top, she lay back on the bed, linked her fingers on her stomach and thought, with relief, that at least he hadn't known about her great seduction plans for the evening. Should she pursue that? she wondered, frowning, or should she just trust that his judgement was sharp enough to see through Philippa? Could she take the chance? More to the point, was she wildly off target in imagining for a fleeting sound that her charms, sadly lacking as they were, were anywhere near potent enough to interest him? Or had desperation somehow done away with common sense?

Why was it, she thought with a sigh, that there was always some mysterious Factor X which seemed to crop up just when things appeared to be going smoothly?

She removed her top, pulling it over her head, and it joined the skirt on the floor.

Lying perfectly straight, she looked down critically at her body, and in the forgiving lack of light she didn't think that she was in too bad a shape. She was naturally thin, boyishly built rather than voluptuous, and her breasts, which admittedly could have done with a couple more inches, matched her frame so that the whole was perfectly in proportion.

She was still staring, musing, when the bedroom door was pushed open.

There was a split-second delay between realisation and horror as Nick walked into the room, during which time, instead of reaching for her T-shirt, she froze.

'I just thought that I'd drop in to see how you were doing.' His voice sounded odd and she sprang into life, grabbing the T-shirt and covering herself inadequately with it.

'You could have knocked.'

'Yes.' He was standing at the foot of the bed and she wished that the mattress would open up and engulf her. He was staring, staring, and making no move towards the door.

'If you don't mind...' she said in a choked voice.

He moved, but not to where she had expected. He moved to the side of the bed and sat down.

'You have a wonderful body,' he muttered huskily. 'Let me see it again.'

Angela gripped the T-shirt tighter and wondered briefly whether she was hallucinating. Perhaps the twisted ankle was somehow affecting her brain patterns. She blinked, saw that he was still sitting there, on the side of the bed, depressing it with his weight, and watched, mesmerised, as his hand covered hers, stroking it.

Her fingers relaxed.

'That was a very appealing outfit you were wearing tonight,' he murmured. 'Was it for me?'

'Naturally not!' Angela lied hotly. 'Why would you think that?'

'Because you don't normally stay up, yet tonight you did, and because you don't normally wear short skirts and tight tops, but tonight you did.' He was still stroking her hand, the hand that was gripping the T-shirt—though less tightly now.

Angela didn't say anything. Struck dumb, she supposed, by the blinding accuracy of his deductions. Did that show uncanny perceptiveness on his part, or massive conceit?

He trailed his finger along the edge of the T-shirt, which was loosely covering her torso. Where the T-shirt stopped and her thighs began he continued trailing his finger, and her body quickened in unconscious response.

She couldn't take her eyes off him. They were locked with his like someone under a spell. She could feel moisture between her thighs at his slow, deliberate arousal.

When his finger touched her through her underwear she gasped but she didn't pull back. He parted her legs, watching her all the time, and slipped his hand under her briefs, cupping her, then rubbing her with his finger until her breathing thickened and she had to close her eyes. Her body had a life of its own, or it seemed to, because she felt herself moving against his finger, twisting her lips, groaning, and she covered her face with her arm and clenched her fist as the rhythmic movements of finger against body grew deeper.

'Don't run away from me this time, Angela,' he whispered into her ear, and she shook her head, really more intent on what he was doing to her body than on what he was saying.

He lay on the bed beside her, and his hand continued to arouse her, taking her higher and higher so that she whimpered.

He didn't have to remove the T-shirt from her because

she did that herself, urgently needing more of her body to be stimulated, arching up for her nipple to meet the wetness of his mouth.

She had a peculiar feeling of being absorbed by him as he sucked her breast, and she turned to face him, unbuttoning his shirt with trembling fingers while their lips met in a hungry, savage kiss. She was moaning uncontrollably while her hands continued the frantic work of undressing him, and when he was naked she reached down and held him, stroking him as he had stroked her, loving the husky breathing that her actions aroused.

This was nice. Being stroked, touched with gentle exploration. She lay back as he resumed his caresses with his mouth, covering her stomach with kisses, moving lower to where his exploring tongue found the core of her womanhood.

Angela groaned and squirmed against his mouth. She felt as though he was drawing her soul out of her into him. When she opened her eyes and saw his dark head moving she felt a stab of desire, a wild rush of feeling that blotted out all clear thought.

She wanted this. It felt right, and so different from that time when Simon had forced himself against her, taken what he had wanted, what he had felt had been his due. He had been an animal, fuelled by anger. Nick was gentle, unhurried, taking his time. An expert, she thought to herself, a man who knew how to give as well as how to receive, but it didn't bother her.

When he parted her legs, she eagerly waited for that final act in their lovemaking. She wanted him so much. It didn't occur to her that there might be a problem, but as soon as he began moving into her she felt her body stiffen, imperceptibly at first, and she forced herself to relax.

But it was impossible. As soon as that little tentacle of fear had taken root it began to throw out its shoots in every direction, and she heard herself telling him to stop, that she couldn't. She felt her body withdrawing from him, and she was trembling when he turned her to face him.

'What is it?' There was no accusation in his voice but she still couldn't meet his eyes. She knew what would follow now. This was going to be a replay of what had happened before—except that it would be a thousand times worse because he would never be able to accept her refusal, not again.

'I'm sorry,' she whispered. Her eyes were wide open, staring at his chest, while her body went into deep freeze mode.

'Is this a game? You pulled away from me once before and you won't be doing it again—not until you explain yourself.' He held onto her shoulders and she squeezed her eyes shut. There was hard intent in his voice rather than biting aggression, but she still couldn't open her mouth. It seemed to be stuffed with cotton wool, and her body was still suffused with panic.

'Are you a virgin?' he asked quietly, and she shook her head. 'Then what the hell is it?'

'I'm sorry, it's just that...' To explain what she had never voiced to anyone in her life before seemed, just then, such an awesome task that she lapsed back into silence. Eventually she opened her eyes and looked at him. She would tell him. She had to. Not because she felt that he needed an explanation, though she supposed that he did, but because suddenly she wanted to. She wanted to share that part of herself with him.

Just him, she thought, because I love him. A thousand disjointed puzzle-pieces slotted into place. Everything could now be explained. Her nerves whenever she was around him—which she had put down to wariness at first, then later to simple physical attraction. The way he played on her mind all the time. The way she responded to him. He doesn't love me but I am deeply in love with him.

'Well?' he asked, and she realised that she had been wrapped up in her thoughts, wrapped up in this new emotion that had been hot enough to melt the ice that surrounded her.

'I can't make love,' she said in a barely audible voice. 'I block off when it reaches... You see...a long time ago, there was a man...' Her voice threatened to peter out altogether. It was an effort to carry on—like trying to stay awake when your eyelids were shutting.

'Tell me,' he murmured. He stroked the hair away from her face and she felt safe. Why, she thought uselessly, did I have to fall in love with the wrong man? What justice was there in that? Had destiny decided, from the day that she was born, to litter her life with insurmountable obstacles? Was that it?

'It was my fault... I was very young and inexperienced and I must have given him ideas...must have led him on. I didn't realise...'

'He raped you.'

Just hearing the word brought the nightmare rushing back, and she felt his hands tighten on her.

'Was he charged?'

'What would have been the point?' She rolled onto her back and stared up at the ceiling. 'The damage had already been done.' He had already left his lifelong legacy, she thought.

'When did this happen?'

'I was just seventeen.' It was getting easier to talk

about it now. 'A very young seventeen. I had always had my head in books, you see. He was the first.'

'Look at me,' Nick said, and she obediently looked at him. 'You can't let this control your life. You have to let it go. It wasn't your fault. He was a bastard, and you can't allow one action of a man like that to blight your responses now or he'll forever have control over you. You have to let it go.'

His voice was soothing. She nodded and touched him very delicately. I have let go, she thought. At last. Because of you.

She let him kiss her, then closed her eyes and felt the freedom of making love for the very first time.

CHAPTER EIGHT

'How do I look?' Angela, eyeing herself in the mirror, shifted her gaze slightly so that she was looking at Natasha, sprawled on the bed with her feet crossed at the ankles. Shoes still on, despite requests to remove them.

'All right.'

'*Just* all right?'

'What does it matter? It's just some stupid dinner with Uncle Nick. You could go wearing a sheet and he probably wouldn't notice.' She was sulky because she had been promised a trial run with oil paints which Angela had had to cancel because Nick had asked her to go with him to a company do.

'Am I the best you can do?' Angela had asked, half teasing to cover her elation at his invitation. For the past week she had felt as though she was walking on air. She was in love and she had her daughter. If there were clouds behind the silver linings, then she had no intention of seeing them. It was enough that Nick wanted her, and if love was not a word that seemed to exist in his vocabulary then so be it. Now, with this invitation, she knew that she was at least not a secret which he wanted to keep hidden away from public view.

'It's very short,' Natasha was saying. 'Aren't you a bit old to be wearing something that short?'

'I'm only in my mid-twenties!' Angela protested,

laughing, and Natasha rolled her eyes and remarked that that was ancient.

She felt absolutely wonderful, though. Her eyes sparkled and there was a flush on her cheeks which had not been there before.

And the dress—polka-dots—with the shoes—very high—looked good. Transformed her, she thought. From schoolteacher to attractive young woman. Or maybe love was behind that particular transformation.

'I've told Eva that you're to go to bed at exactly nine o'clock,' Angela said, sitting on the bed and looking at Natasha with as firm an expression as she could muster.

'I think it's very unfair of Uncle Nick to expect you to go to some boring old party with him at a minute's notice. Where's Philippa? She usually forces herself along to these things.'

'Philippa,' Angela said lightly, 'is in America on holiday.' She bent and kissed Natasha on the forehead. They seemed more and more natural, these little shows of affection. 'Don't give Eva a hard time. Go to bed when she tells you to.'

'Or else...?' Natasha raised her eyebrows challengingly and Angela laughed.

'Or else I shall...' She searched for a suitable threat, couldn't find one, and said limply, 'I shall be terribly disappointed.'

'I hate threats like that,' Natasha complained, which made Angela laugh again.

It was getting harder to remember those years spent in limbo, unhappy, unable to trust. Memories were becoming less precise. Very gradually they were being put away, one by one. Her childhood, her father, Simon, the loss of her daughter, the years of pain. They were still there but they were no longer part of her daily life.

She left Natasha in the bedroom, grabbing her bag on the way out, and by the time she had made her way down the staircase Nick was waiting for her at the bottom.

He looked up as she walked down. Would the thrill of seeing him ever wane? she wondered. Did sheer physical beauty ever lose its lustre? He was formally dressed in a black dinner suit, and she half smiled at the thought that she knew that muscular body almost as well as she knew her own.

'How do I look?' she asked, when she had reached the bottom and was standing next to him.

'Edible.' He touched her breast and smiled as he felt her nipple harden in response. She hadn't worn a bra because the back of her dress was cut too low, and she had a fleeting image of him scooping her breast out, caressing it with his mouth. Would it be as erotic an experience for him as it would for her?

'Is the taxi here?' she asked and he nodded.

'Unfortunately. Although,' he mused, opening the front door, 'if we were to do what I want right now, we'd probably end up arriving at the hotel just as the whole thing was winding up.'

'Not a good idea considering you are the Big Bad Boss,' Angela laughed.

They didn't talk much in the taxi, just throwaway remarks about nothing in particular, but he held her hand and stroked her thumb, and it was all she could do not to let him see how warm the gesture made her feel.

She couldn't risk showing him her feelings. She knew that that would be a mistake. For the moment his suspicions of her were in abeyance, overridden by desire, but if she sparkled too much, revealed emotions which should remain hidden, then all those suspicions would rise to the surface again, like scum finding its natural level.

She had no idea where all this was going to lead, and whenever she made an effort to determine its destination she felt overwhelmed by a vague sense of desperation. So she tried not to think about it.

I'm a coward, she admitted to herself. But why shouldn't I snatch some happiness for myself? For once.

The hotel was busy when they arrived. They were escorted to the privately booked room and she felt a twinge of nervousness as she looked around at the assorted crowd, milling about with drinks in their hands.

There seemed to be a sea of people—hundreds. Nick had told her that the entire company had been invited, along with their other halves.

Within ten seconds she could work out how the groups were split. The younger ones were standing for the most part all together, while the older members were in smaller groups, and probably, she thought, subdivided into management levels.

It was only after she had done her mental survey that she realised to what extent she was an object of curiosity herself. More so as Nick tucked her arm into his and began mingling with the crowd.

He had a phenomenal recall for names and they worked their way around the room methodically.

'I think,' she whispered to him, smiling, 'that you have quite an effect on the ladies here.'

'Now, I wonder what you mean?' His mouth curved with amusement and he inclined slightly towards her so that he could hear her above the general din of voices vying to be heard.

She could smell him. A clean, masculine smell, free from any aftershave or cologne. His arm, through his jacket, was hard, muscular. He exuded power and a peculiar magnetism that made people aware of his presence even, apparently, when their backs were to him. Was it any wonder that some of the younger girls had stammered and blushed when he casually stopped to say something to them? Was it any wonder that she, herself, had run the gauntlet of veiled, interested inspection?

It appeared that the older the member of staff the more covert was the inspection, and by the time they found themselves at the far corner of the room, with a group of men who turned out to be directors of various parts of the company, Angela was not aware of any interest in her apart from the strictly polite variety.

She found herself relaxing, only then realising how aware she had been of the very public examination of her, and enjoying herself enough to laugh and chat without feeling stiff and self-conscious.

'Now,' Nick murmured to her later, when the meal was finished, speeches had been made, and people were dispersing to various connecting rooms in which entertainment of various kinds had been laid on, 'that wasn't too bad, was it?'

They headed away from the action, and out through doors to the garden, which was empty. It seemed that the stillness of nature at night was no competition for the disco, the casino or the bar. Most of the older generation, having put in an appearance, had left, and the younger crowd could be seen through the doors, laughing with considerably more abandon now that they were no longer under the eyes of upper management.

Angela laughed. 'Of course, they'll all be wondering, Who exactly *is* she? I mean, it's hardly as if they've seen my face around the office. They'll think that you've pulled me out of nowhere, like a conjuror pulling a rabbit out of a hat.' She looked up at him and caught an odd glint in his eyes.

'Perhaps if they arrive at an answer they could share it with me,' he said, looking straight down at her.

Angela looked back at him anxiously, wondering whether this was a prelude to suspicions which would spoil the pleasantness between them.

He read her mind. 'You're frowning.' He placed his hands on her shoulders. 'You have that look of a frightened animal caught in someone's headlights. Why?'

'I'm not frightened.' She dropped her eyes. 'I just hate it when you start questioning me.'

'There's a difference between asking questions and questioning. Questioning implies cross-examination.' He tilted her face up, one finger under her chin. 'Who are you? Really?'

'You know who I am.'

'Do I?' He smiled drily. 'You're the most elusive woman I've ever met in my life. I can touch you, but there's some part of you that I seem incapable of reaching. It's like trying to catch a wisp of smoke.'

That all sounded vaguely romantic, as though, she thought, there was some enigma about her. It was ironic, considering how very tangible her secret was, and it was also ironic considering that he had reached deep enough inside her to waken in her this miracle of love.

'Is that why you...?'

'Why I...what?'

'Why you're attracted to me?' she asked in a small voice. It seemed strange voicing the concept, as though saying it aloud might dissipate it. 'Because you see me as some sort of personal challenge? Because you don't think that I'm straightforward?'

'What do you think?'

'I think,' she answered, taking a deep breath, 'that we should go back inside, where you can keep an eye on your unruly members of staff.' They both looked back towards the room and he laughed under his breath.

'They do seem to be enjoying themselves, don't they?' he murmured, with a note of indulgence in his voice, and some of the tension eased out of her as she realised that, for whatever reason, he had chosen not to pursue the uncomfortable topic of her elusiveness.

'They'll all be suffering from tremendous hangovers in the morning,' she pointed out.

'Tut, tut, you're beginning to slip into your prim schoolteacher mode.'

Angela looked up at him and grinned. 'It's a hard habit to break.'

'Now, there's another challenge,' he said with amusement. 'Breaking you of that bad habit.'

She felt a hot glow invade her, and she had to stop herself from imagining what it would be like to be loved by him, with an endless, proprietorial love that would fill her. It would be like soaring upwards into the clouds.

'Let's head in,' she said, sighing.

'But first...' He turned her to him, his head descended and his mouth met hers in a kiss. She wound her arms around his neck, pulling him to her, sinking into the pleasurable feeling of tongue against tongue.

'Hello, Nick.'

The harsh sound of Philippa's voice was enough of a shock to make her jerk away, and they both turned to see her standing by them, arms folded.

'I can see I'm interrupting something,' she said acidly, which immediately made Angela want to rush into instant denial.

But before she could utter a word, Nick said smoothly,

'Yes, you are, as a matter of fact. I thought you were in America until next Monday, Philippa.' There was an edge of cold steel to his voice, but it was lost on Philippa, who remained where she was with a look of fury on her face.

'I came back early so that I could try and make it to this do! Little did I know that I'd arrive to find you…to find you in the dark, entwined with the…the hired help!'

Nick didn't raise his voice. 'I think you've said quite enough. I suggest you leave before I lose my temper.'

Angela thought that it sounded very much as though he had already lost it, but Philippa was either immune to that fact or else her rage was consuming enough for her to throw caution to the winds.

'How could you, Nick?' She adopted a wheedling tone, but her body was still as rigid as stone. 'We had something once. You asked me to come and work for you over here…you led me to believe—'

'I led you to believe nothing, Philippa,' he replied coldly. 'You volunteered to come over here and I accepted because you know the workings of the company and you're good at your job. If you read any more into it than that, then I'm afraid you misunderstood the situation completely.'

There was a silence after this which seemed desperately long. Philippa's stunning face was contorted with emotion—not, Angela suspected, grief, but anger at plans which had been frustrated.

'You felt nothing for me, did you, Nick?'

'I felt precisely what you felt for me. Now I think it's time we brought this conversation to an end.'

'Well, I don't!' Her eyes fell on Angela, who had been trying to make herself as invisible as she could. 'I see you've been taking your best clothes out of the closet,' she said scathingly. Her mouth twisted into an ugly parody of a smile and she looked at Nick. 'Are you so blind that you can't see what this…this tramp is trying to do?'

She gave a snort of unpleasant laughter. 'She's swanned into your life on some trumped-up story of having known your sister, inveigled herself into the household, and now she's got what she wanted. An affair with you! Don't tell me that you can't see exactly what she's after! She's nothing but a gold-digger!'

Angela felt her face burn with outrage.

'Goodbye, Philippa,' was all that Nick said to this. 'I suggest you clear your office before I get there on Tuesday.'

'You can't sack me!'

'I already have.'

'This is all your fault,' Philippa hissed, stepping towards Angela, who immediately felt a flare of sheer panic surge through her. 'You'll be sorry.'

She turned and left, half running, drawing far fewer curious glances from the young people milling about in the room than she would have earlier on, if she had arrived before the drink had done its work.

She vanished and Angela remained stiffly rooted to the spot. She didn't dare look at Nick. Philippa's accusations were ringing in her ears—as they must be in his as well. Gold-digger. A nasty word.

'I think it's time we went in,' he said finally, in the sort of voice that gave no clues as to what he was thinking, and Angela felt a wave of misery flow over her and then subside.

'Of course. What time do you plan to leave?'

They were heading back inside and she kept her eyes firmly fastened in front of her.

'The bar closes in under an hour. People should start leaving then. We should be back home in a couple of hours. Makes it a very long evening, but as the head of this company I think I ought to stay and see it through. Would you like me to call a taxi for you?'

They were skirting around the subject and she was horribly and depressingly aware of his politeness. This was what it felt like to come plummeting back to earth. It hurt.

She shook her head. 'No, no. It's all right. I'll stay on until you're ready to leave.'

'Sure?'

She nodded and followed him through to the disco. The crowd there was already thinning out and, as he had predicted, a further surge of people departed shortly after the bar closed.

They sat at a table at the back, with the music tapering off in the background. Vigorous songs had given way to slow ballads. In a short while the band would pack up and it would be time to leave. And still nothing had been said about Philippa.

'I'm afraid Philippa's appearance lent a rather unpleasant note to the proceedings,' he said eventually, facing her across the table. He nodded at a couple behind her, on their way out, and then returned to watch her.

'Yes, it did.'

'She was extremely foolish to harbour illusions about us ever getting back together.' His voice was flat and matter-of-fact.

'People do,' Angela told him, painfully aware of how truthful the words were. 'Sometimes they don't mean to.'

'I'm quite sure that Philippa was well aware of what she was doing.' He looked at her narrowly. 'She thought that I was up for grabs and she was wrong.'

'Are you telling me this by way of explanation or by way of warning, Nick?' She took a deep breath and hung onto her courage while it was still there. 'Do you think that I'm after your money?'

'It makes sense, wouldn't you agree?' He shrugged and looked away towards the group of musicians, who were now efficiently packing away their paraphernalia.

'Why does it make sense?'

'Philippa took me for a fool. I suggest you don't make the same mistake.' He glanced at her, and in the darkness of the room she wondered whether his eyes were as un-revealing as his voice.

I am the fool, she thought, but not for the reasons you suspect. I'm a fool to have fallen in love with you.

'The first time I came near you, you ran a mile. After what you subsequently told me, I assumed that sheer fear of sexual intercourse had made you take flight, but there could be another explanation, couldn't there? You could simply have given the matter a little thought—decided that there were limitless options open to you because of my attraction to you. At which point perhaps you thought that a little seduction might not go amiss.' He was quite conversational about it, as though they were simply dis-cussing the weather.

'Hence,' he continued, 'your sudden overtures of friendliness. Waiting up for me to hear what kind of day I'd had at work. And then, of course, we slept together, which implies that whatever fears your past experience may have generated, you managed to overcome them. Why? Or why all of a sudden? I should ask.'

'Would you be asking me these questions now if it weren't for Philippa?'

'Possibly not,' he said calmly. 'But that doesn't mean that it hasn't crossed my mind.'

He glanced at his watch and stood up, and Angela followed suit. She had the dizzy feeling of someone who had been happily sailing along on calm water, only to find themselves suddenly in the middle of a raging hurricane. So what, she wondered, happens now? Several possibilities sprang to mind, and none of them were very pleasant. She walked with him back out into the main room, now cleared of stragglers, feeling sick and wretched.

Their taxi was outside, waiting for them.

There was no point in talking about this in the back seat of a taxi. It was too personal a subject to be aired in the presence of a third party. Nick clearly felt the same because he made indifferent conversation about the party, asking her what she'd thought of the food, the entertainment, and she heard herself replying in a fractured voice while her mind obsessively played over and over what he had said earlier.

After a while they lapsed into silence, and it was only when they were back at the house, and a sleeping Eva had been roused and sent on her way home, that she turned to him and said stiffly, 'Is that really what you thought from the start? That I was a gold-digger? That my whole purpose of being here was to…to find a way of…'

He leaned casually against the wall and looked at her. 'I was prepared to give you the benefit of the doubt at first, but it wouldn't be the first time that a woman has tried to get to my bank balance by way of my bed. As I've told you before, I have quite a bit of experience in that particular field. Enough to recognise the warning bells.'

'Fine. If that's what you think, then that's fine.' She turned away, but before she could walk off his hand snaked out and gripped her wrist.

'Don't turn your back on me in the middle of a conversation,' he grated, and she glared at him.

'Why not?' Angela asked recklessly. 'You can simply add "rude" to your list of other pleasant adjectives.'

She wished that he would let her go. Her head was sending messages of anger through her but her body was responding to the feel of his fingers against her skin, and she hated that sense of vulnerability, that feeling of being caught in the grip of a passion over which she had no power.

She thought of Natasha, asleep upstairs in her bed, and forced herself to calm down.

'Why don't you try and deny that you're after my money?' he asked, with a curious lack of rancour.

'Why should I? I've tried before, and it's pointless trying to deny anything when you've plainly already made up your mind.'

'Try me,' he said softly. 'Feel free to tell me that, despite a string of coincidences, the only thing that motivated you to sleep with me was attraction. That there's no ulterior motive behind your presence in my house.'

Angela looked down at the tips of her shoes. They would need a clean. They no longer looked elegant and vaguely alluring. In fact, they looked rather sad. She was glad that she was wearing a jacket over her polka-dot dress, because she knew that if she looked at that it would seem rather sad as well.

'You can't, can you?' he said calmly. 'No, I didn't think so. Then why don't you admit that you were only ever after my money? That way, you could say that we've cleared the air.'

'I would rather just go to bed, if you don't mind. We can discuss this in the morning, when we're—'

'We'll discuss it now!'

The harshness of his voice made her head snap up and she stared at him with alarm.

'There's nothing I feel I can say,' she told him, bravely meeting his eyes for about three seconds, then looking away.

'Damn you!' His eyes glittered in the shadowy hallway. His hold tightened on her wrist. 'Why don't you come clean? Are you after my money?'

'No!' The admission was wrenched out of her but it didn't make her feel any better. He wanted the truth from her, and that was the truth, but it didn't free her from deceit. She was simply concealing deceit of a different nature. 'I'm not after your money,' she whispered. 'I don't care about your money! And anyway why did you...were you prepared to make love to me if you thought that I was?'

'Why do you think?' He reached behind her neck, pulling her towards him, kissing her with such force that her head tilted back under the impact. His tongue moved inside her mouth, demanding, punishing, and she squirmed against him in an attempt to free herself from the embrace.

He was not about to let her go, though. He continued to kiss her and she fought the yearning to respond with every ounce of her will-power.

'I want you,' he muttered thickly against her mouth. He cupped her face with one hand. 'It appears to override other considerations.'

She felt a swift rush of pleasure, immediately followed by the bleak realisation that she was caught in a situation from which she had to extricate herself. Forthwith. He wanted her, and for a few heady days she had been too blinded by love to see the path she was heading down.

The cold reality was that desire and lust were passing

emotions, and as soon as he tired of her he would rapidly come to the conclusion that her presence was no longer tolerable. She would have outstayed her welcome.

Wasn't that what ex-mistresses finally became? Embarrassments to be hustled out of the doorway so that their floor space could be filled sooner or later by someone else?

If she had had nothing to lose but her pride, then she realised that she would have carried on. She would have played his game, lost herself in love and taken the eventual consequences. She could have lived with the hurt more easily than she could have lived with the regret.

But life was never as straightforward as that and she had much more to lose than her pride.

She placed her hands flat on his chest and pushed him, turning her head aside, blinking very rapidly so that her emotions could not rise to the surface and undermine her.

'I can't see this through,' she said, realising with horror that she sounded far more emotional than she looked.

He stepped back, shoved his hands in his pockets and gave her a frustrated, angry look.

'Tell me why. You say that you're not after my money. You're as attracted to me as I am to you. Where's the problem?'

The problem? she thought bitterly. Where is it? It's everywhere! It doesn't matter where I turn, I just end up crashing into it, and burying my head in the sand isn't going to make it go away—it's just going to make it even more unbearable to face when the time comes.

'How can you expect me to have a relationship with you—to sleep with you,' she amended, 'knowing that you think those things about me? How do you imagine that makes me feel about myself?'

She raised her eyes to his and felt, with misery, as

though she was looking at him for the last time. She would see him again, but never in a situation as intimate as this.

'If I told you that I believed you, would that change things?' His voice was harsh, as though the words were being dragged out of him, and there was a dull, angry flush on his cheeks.

'No.'

'None of this would have happened if Philippa hadn't appeared on the scene.'

'It would have, sooner or later.' When I came to my senses, she thought, which would probably have been sooner rather than later. 'You're not a man who's going to commit himself to a relationship. I know that. Maybe, for a while, I thought that I could be the same, but perhaps I want something more for myself. I don't know.'

Angela looked at him steadily. There was a lot that she wasn't telling him, that she *couldn't* tell him, but that at least was true. She wanted more out of him than sex— or rather, she knew that she would in the end. And she was prepared to tell him so, knowing very well that on that score he would never succumb.

Nick Cameron wasn't born to be caged. Oh, doubtless he would get married in the fullness of time, but never because he had been swept off his feet by a woman. No, she imagined that when he married it would be because he had thought it through and had made his choice based on far more prosaic factors, like social and intellectual and financial compatibility.

He was ruthlessly self-controlled. She didn't think that it was possible for him to shed that because of a woman. It would be like telling a shark to buckle down and start acting like a guppy.

'What, exactly, are you telling me here, Angela?' he

grated, and she shrugged, which seemed to antagonise him further, because his dark eyebrows met in a savage frown.

'I'm not sure that I know,' she admitted honestly. 'The only thing I know is that we're not getting anywhere with this conversation and it's time we both went to bed. It's late. Natasha is going to be up bright and early in the morning because I promised to teach her about using oils, and I need some sleep or else I shall get up tomorrow like a zombie.'

'We're not ending this conversation until it's reached a conclusion.'

'It *has* reached a conclusion!'

'Not one that I'm satisfied with!'

They stared at each other in silence, and Angela frankly didn't know which way to turn. Her secret lay between them like a yawning chasm which only she could see.

'What sort of commitment do you want from me?' he asked in a controlled voice. 'A promise that we'll keep this thing going for three weeks? Three months? Three years? There are no guarantees in life!'

'I know that, and I'm not asking anything from you.'

'Or do you want that band of gold on your finger?' he continued softly, ignoring her input. 'Is that the sort of commitment you're looking for? Marriage?'

He was watching her closely. She could feel the weight of those hypnotic grey eyes pressing down on her like lead.

'No. You don't understand.'

'Are you telling me that if I asked you to marry me, you would refuse?' There was no element of proposition in his voice, more of cynical speculation, as though he was raising a hypothetical question simply out of curiosity.

'I'm telling you,' Angela said, 'that if you asked me to marry you, I would refuse.'

The silence that greeted this was so complete that she seemed to hear it, a thick, flat lack of noise that was as resounding as a roomful of sound. His eyes were hooded, expressionless. A closed book. She wondered what her own face was revealing about herself. She would have liked to have that talent for pulling the shutters down, but she didn't, and so she looked away from him.

'All I really want,' she continued after a while, almost as though there had been no break in the conversation, 'is for things to go back to being as they were.'

She held her breath, waiting for the inevitable cynicism that would greet this statement. Even to herself it sounded impossibly naïve. How on earth could things go back to being as they were? Unless they jointly suffered an attack of amnesia that blotted out what had taken place between them over the past week or so. The full extent of the hole which she had dug for herself opened out in front of her. A huge, black, gaping hole that was waiting to engulf her.

In her head, she began planning what she would do if he gave her the sack. He couldn't *make* her stop seeing Natasha. She would move permanently to London, somewhere close, get a job at a school, see her daughter at every conceivable opportunity.

'Fine,' he said in a cold, clipped voice. 'I have never begged for a woman in my life and I don't intend to start now.'

Angela released a sigh of relief. 'Thank you. Thank you,' she whispered, not daring to look at him just in case he had a change of heart.

She turned away and walked up the staircase, then, when she was out of sight, she ran to her room and shut the door behind her, leaning heavily against it in the dark. For how long, she had no idea. She heard him follow her up the stairs, then his footsteps vanished as he headed for his bedroom. Only then did she creep out, out to Natasha's room. Just to have one look at her before she went to sleep.

It was a nightly check that had become a habit. Sometimes in the middle of the night, if she got up to go to the bathroom, she would tiptoe along the corridor, push the door open and have a peep at her sleeping, unaware daughter. Just to make sure.

She silently went to the bedroom, pushed open the door—and her mind went completely blank. The bed was empty, the bedclothes thrown to one side.

She raced to the bathroom. Empty. She could feel her heart beating wildly inside her. Desperation replaced panic and she rushed upstairs to Nick's bedroom and banged on his door.

'It's Natasha,' she said hysterically when he was standing in front of her, still fully dressed with the exception of his jacket and his bow tie. 'She's gone!'

CHAPTER NINE

'WHAT,' Nick asked coolly, 'are you talking about?'

'Natasha's gone.' She lost the edge of hysteria in her voice, although her heart was still beating wildly. 'I went to her bedroom to check on her—I do most nights—and she's not there. Her bedclothes are everywhere!'

'Where else did you look for her?'

'The bathroom. She's not there.'

He went outside, onto the small landing, then down the stairs to the second floor, and shouted, 'Natasha!' so loudly that Angela jumped.

They waited for a few seconds, listening to the reverberating silence that greeted this, then he said in a clipped voice, 'Right. You check this floor; I'll look downstairs. She's probably in the kitchen, pouring herself some milk, or maybe she's fallen asleep in one of the rooms downstairs.'

'Eva...'

'Was sound asleep when we arrived back.'

'Perhaps we should phone her...' She could feel sweaty panic creeping back and she tried to force it down. Panic wasn't going to solve anything, and anyway Nick was probably right. As babysitters went, Eva was a pretty passive presence in the house. Heaven only knew what time she had nodded off. Natasha could easily have been unable to get to sleep, sneaked down to the library and fallen asleep in front of a book. If she had thought about it logically, she would have checked the entire house before rousing Nick, but logic had flown out of the window the minute she had seen that empty bed.

'We'll look around first.' He headed off downstairs, taking them two at a time, and Angela began searching the upstairs rooms. Three bathrooms, a huge TV room, which had originally been used as a snooker room, the bedrooms, under the beds.

Her own bedroom was the last that she checked, basically because it was geographically at the very end of the house, and as soon as she switched on the bedroom light she began to have a sickening premonition of what had happened.

There was no Natasha there. Everything was as she had left it earlier on. The wardrobe doors were shut, the drawers of the chest were closed, but there was a small bundle of papers on the middle of the bed—well positioned so that the minute the light was switched on they were instantly noticeable.

Angela walked very slowly towards the bed, but she knew precisely what they were before she picked them up. Letters, photos of Natasha growing up, which she had treasured from one year to the next, everything that told the story of the adoption. Everything.

There was hardly any point in looking further. She could guess at what had happened. Hadn't Philippa said that she would be sorry? She must have made her way here as soon as that unpleasant scene had concluded. Eva would have let her in without thinking twice because she knew Philippa. It would have taken the filmiest of excuses to get into the house. What had she told Eva? What had been her excuse for entering the house at such a late hour?

Had she said that she had returned to fetch some work

papers? Something that Nick had forgotten, which she had volunteered to return for? His wallet, perhaps? There were a hundred vaguely plausible excuses she could have used, and Eva might have clucked her tongue in irritation at being roused but she would have given her free rein, returned to the sitting room and dozed off again probably, giving her all the time in the world to do her worst. Not that it would have taken much time.

Angela had hidden all those private documents, but not under lock and key. She had never for a minute thought that anyone would have any reason to go through her things. They had been in the bottom drawer of the chest of drawers, tucked away at the back inside an old diary, years old, lovingly kept to record everything that she had felt, thought, done in the first few dreadful months after she had handed Natasha over.

She held the little cluster of papers in her hand, turning it over, then she went downstairs.

There was more urgency in Nick's face as he appeared in the hall.

'Any luck?' he asked, looking up at her, and she shook her head. 'Where the hell could she be?' he exploded.

Angela took a deep breath and said quietly. 'I think we should go and sit down. There's something I need to tell you.'

'Can't it wait?'

'It has a bearing on what may be going on with your niece, Nick.'

He looked at her more carefully this time, then he nodded and walked towards the sitting room. Angela followed him. Her feet felt like lead and she had reached that peculiar stage where panic had disappeared, the adrenaline had stopped flowing completely, and all that was left was a numb sense of the inevitable.

Wasn't that what they said about people who were staring extreme danger in the face? Their minds shut down completely in a self-defence mechanism when desperation and fear could no longer be absorbed.

'You look as though you could do with a drink,' he said when they were both in the sitting room, facing each other. 'Do you know what's going on?'

'I think so. Yes. Yes, I do.' She still had the little parcel in her hands and she compulsively played with it, turning it over, smoothing it down, feeling its texture against her fingers. She reached out and handed it to him. 'I think you should read this.'

His eyes flicked from the parcel to her face. It was a little while before he took it from her and there was another pause before he looked down at it.

He started with the diary. She had never shown anyone that diary in her life before. She herself had read and reread it so many times that she knew the entries virtually off by heart. For the first few months she had written something in it every day, recording her thoughts, then later there had been fewer entries, sometimes just a sentence or so.

He read them in silence, his body very still, then he turned over the bundle of papers and began looking through them, one by one, very carefully. When he had finished he read them all again, as though having to verify what he had already seen for himself. Then he looked up at her and said, with ice in his voice. 'I see.'

'I think Philippa returned here and went through my drawers. I don't suppose she had any idea what she was looking for, but she has been suspicious of me from the start. Just as you were.'

'With good cause, as it transpires,' Nick told her, with

such contemptuous dislike that she felt the muscles in her face stiffen.

'I think that she found my...my past, woke Natasha and told her. I don't suppose she thought that Natasha would run away, but she knew that everything...that I would have lost...' She couldn't go on. Not without breaking down. She stopped talking, looked down at her hands and made an effort to compose herself. 'Natasha's run away. We need to try and work out where she may have gone.'

She thought of her daughter, cowering somewhere, angry and scared. Well, time enough to cope with all her own inevitable emotions. Right now, the most important thing was to try and find her.

'I have a list of all the children in her class,' she said, standing up and moving towards the telephone on the table by the bay window. She flipped through a flowered notebook by the phone, extracted a pink sheet of paper and walked across to hand it to him. 'I think you should call them.'

He took the paper without looking at her.

He hates me so much, she thought, that he can't even bear to look at my face. He suspected that I was after his money. This deception must be far, far worse.

He started at the top of the list. 'I'm very sorry to disturb you at this hour...I have a bit of a problem on my hands...it seems that my niece...'

It was easy to follow what the reactions were at the other end. Irritation at being wakened in the early hours of the morning, surprise at the request, an anxious check to make sure that their own daughter had not done something silly with Natasha, then polite concern mixed with relief that their own child was safely tucked up in bed, and sympathetic promises to call immediately if Natasha arrived on their doorstep.

Angela sat perched on the arm of a chair, watching Nick's back as he methodically made his way down the list. One negative response after another, until the list was completed, then he turned to her and said, 'Have you any suggestions as to where else we could check?' He didn't wait for her response. He called Eva, his questions clipped, and when he had finished talking, he turned to her.

'It appears that you were right about Philippa. She must have come here as soon as she left the hotel. Eva says that she neither saw nor heard Natasha from the moment she put her to bed at a little after eight-thirty.'

'This is my fault,' Angela whispered.

Nick regarded her with a cold lack of sympathy. 'It's pointless trying to apportion blame.'

'I think we ought to call the police.'

It was only after the police had arrived, taken details and spoken to Eva, who had hurried over shortly after her conversation with Nick, arriving on the doorstep in a state of worry tinged with self-recrimination, that Angela went to Nick and said tentatively, 'If I'd been Natasha, I might have felt like running to the one place where I had felt safe. She may have gone to your sister's house.'

The police had left, with assurances that they would do their best, that they should not start panicking now, and Eva had made a pot of tea, which was, at present, going quite cold in the cups on the table in the sitting room.

It was a chance, wasn't it? Nick called the house, and there was no answer.

'I'll drive up.' He started moving towards the door and

Angela raced after him, not caring just then what he thought of her, only knowing that she must go with him.

'I'm coming with you.'

He stopped in his tracks and looked at her fully in the face.

'I don't see any point to that, do you? You are the reason she left in the first place. I don't think that even if she is there confronting you is going to do her any good at all, do you?'

'I don't care what you think! Natasha is my daughter! I'm coming whether you like it or not. If you don't take me with you, I shall just drive behind you.'

She stared at him mutinously, absolutely unyielding, and he turned on his heel and strode off, stopping on the way to tell Eva what was going on, that she was to stay by the telephone in case there was a call.

He didn't once glance back at her, and she thought that she would really have to pile into her car and do her best to tail him, but as she moved to veer off to her car he said harshly, 'Get in! If you must come, then you might just as well come with me. I know the way.'

This time it was no comfortable silence between them. It was thick with unspoken tension. She was beginning to think that it might have been a better idea, after all, to have gone her own way, when he said, with casual distaste, 'So tell me, when did you hatch this little plan of yours?'

He made it sound as though she had been plotting to blow up the Houses of Parliament, and she felt the thick bile of anger rise up in her throat. She swallowed it down.

'You could make an attempt to try and understand—'

'Understand!' He banged his fist against the steering wheel. 'Understand that you lied your way into my house?'

'I had to!'

'You could have tried telling the truth from the start.'

She laughed bitterly at that. 'Tell me how I could have risked that! What makes you think that your reaction would have been any different then from what it is now?' She looked out of the window and contemplated the empty darkness racing past them.

'I know what you think about mothers who give their babies up for adoption,' she said in a more controlled voice, but still keeping her eyes away from his face, because every time he looked at her it was like a knife cutting through her. 'You don't understand because you don't want to, but I was desperately young and naïve, pregnant with a baby conceived in the worst of all possible circumstances, living with an alcoholic father in a council flat that could hardly fit the both of us and his bottles...I was scared stiff. My father said that he would throw me out if I brought the baby back.'

'The council would have housed you.'

'When? They couldn't promise a date, and anyway, was that what I wanted for my baby? A life of poverty and despair—because there would be no way that I could finish my studies. I was still at school! Do you think that it didn't hurt...? Do you imagine that it's ever stopped hurting...? The social worker was very kind, very understanding, and I was so confused. It's hard when you're in a situation so very desperate, with absolutely no one to lean on.' She looked across at him and he shot her a sideways glance.

'Carry on,' he said abruptly, and she wanted to ask him why. Why carry on? So that she could fill the silence? Because he certainly wasn't prepared to sympathise.

'I was introduced to your sister and her husband. I

liked them both and they agreed that I could keep in touch with Natasha. Not directly, but through them. They promised that when she reached her teens they would explain about me, that we could meet. It was one of my conditions of the adoption. I felt as though I wasn't cutting all ties.'

This was hopeless, explaining all this to him. He saw her as a monster, one who had used him to get what she wanted. She almost wished that he would voice it all, so that she could have an opportunity to fight back. How could she ever have felt that this was the one person she might confide in, had the situation been different? She must have been crazy!

'How did you find out about Clive and Amanda's accident?' he asked, with neither compassion nor condemnation in his voice. It was the voice of a stranger.

Angela sighed and decided that she would tell him everything, but without the emotion. She would recite the facts and omit everything else.

'They were very good about keeping in contact,' she said tonelessly. 'And then it dried up. I tried to get in touch, but I couldn't. I didn't think that they would suddenly have decided to stop communicating, so I began checking. I didn't know where Natasha went to school, but I knew that she was privately educated and that it was a local school. I phoned around and I was lucky. The headteacher told me what had happened. She gave me your address. I don't suppose she should have, but I guess it helped that I was a fellow teacher. She even knew the principal at the school where I taught! They had been to university together. So that was how I got in touch with you.'

'And you coolly and cunningly decided what you were going to do.'

She could barely match his description to herself. Cool and cunning were the last things she had been. Desperate and emotional, perhaps, but of course he wouldn't see it that way.

'What made you think that it would work? That I would employ you? Or were you so confident of your own ability to persuade that failure didn't loom on the horizon?' There was acid sarcasm in his voice and she had an insane desire to shake him until he could *see*.

'I had to try. Natasha is my daughter. I didn't expect *anything*, but I prayed.'

'And lo and behold, your prayers were answered!'

They had cleared London now, were picking up speed. He broke off the conversation to call Eva on his carphone, and when he replaced the receiver she knew, without being told, that there was no news.

'I should have listened a bit harder to my instincts,' he muttered grimly. 'I knew there was something odd about your story, something that didn't quite tie up. I let myself be hoodwinked by you.'

And I let myself fall in love with you, she thought, so who's hurting more now?

'Tell me,' he said in a conversational voice that didn't fool her for a minute, 'is there anything genuine about you at all?' He glanced across at her, but she could only see the glitter in his eyes; she couldn't read his expression.

When she didn't reply, he continued, in the slow, musing voice of someone expressing thoughts rather than engaging in debate, 'A gold-digger I could have coped with. Even understood, to some extent. But there is something quite cold and calculating about your nature of deception. And how cleverly you played it. All those moans of pleasure when we made love. A convincing act. Was your eventual ploy to marry me, so that you could finally achieve what you ultimately wanted—namely to be with your daughter without fear of being torn apart from her again? Was it?'

'I told you that I didn't want to marry you,' Angela said woodenly. 'I know what you think of me, but... Oh, what's the use!'

'Call it satisfying my curiosity,' he said with dislike. 'Where did you imagine it would end, Angela? When would you have spilled the beans? When the wedding ring was on your finger, if that was the ultimate goal?'

'I lived from day to day,' she said on a sigh. 'I can't fight with you over this, Nick. I don't blame you for feeling the way that you do...'

'Oh, how thoughtful of you!'

'I realise you think you've been used.'

'A bitter lesson and one that's well learned,' he replied tightly. 'No wonder you wanted to break off our little...escapade together,' he carried on. 'In retrospect, it all makes sense, doesn't it? You fought shy of making love, but you couldn't afford to play too hard to get, could you? I mean, what if I lost interest altogether? So you made yourself available and then played your dramatic card, retreating with wounded pride after Philippa's outburst. You must have imagined that I would pursue you, and, of course, if I had you would have allowed yourself to be pursued—albeit a little reluctantly to start with. And then the gamble. Marriage or no more. Does all this sound a little familiar, Angela?'

'No. You make me sound like—'

'Don't deny a word of it!' The cold composure gave way to harsh fury. 'If I didn't have my hands on the steering wheel,' he said savagely, 'I would shake you until you admitted everything.'

Angela closed her eyes and rested her head back against the car seat. She felt less tired now than she had done earlier on, after they had left the party, but much, much more weary. Her bones ached, her head ached, her eyes were heavy. She would have liked to go to sleep, to escape to some place where she didn't have to listen to Nick's contemptuous judgement of her, but she couldn't even manage to doze.

She had a gut feeling that Natasha was at the house. It was about an hour's drive from London, but if she had wanted to she could easily have sneaked downstairs, called for a taxi and waited outside while Eva blissfully slept on the sofa in the sitting room. Money would not have been a problem. There was money lying around the house: pound coins which Nick randomly flushed out of his pockets and which she, Eva and Natasha had taken to storing away in jars scattered here and there.

She had no idea what she would say or do if and when they found her. It all seemed like an unavoidable nightmare.

She must have dozed a bit, though, because she started when she felt the car slowing down and was wide awake when it pulled up outside a large beamed house set in landscaped grounds.

So this, she thought, is where my daughter lived. She gazed at the house and tried to picture Natasha there, running in the garden—getting *lost* in the garden, it was so huge. She imagined the inside of the house, a network of rooms—small, cosy bedrooms, with floral wallpaper and fireplaces, larger rooms downstairs, beamed and tastefully decorated.

She thought of the council flat where she had grown up, with its cramped rooms that had made you feel like a rabbit trapped in a hutch, the messy kitchen with signs of her father's drink problem everywhere, the small park viewed from above which the council had struggled manfully to maintain against all odds. What would Natasha's fate have been if she had kept her? If she hadn't been so young and gullible? Would love have been able to carry them out of their miserable surroundings? Would it have conquered everything?

She switched the thoughts off and slipped out of the car, following Nick to the front door.

Apart from the porch light, the house looked dark and utterly empty—and it was. They rang the bell, and after several attempts he looked at her and said, 'We'll circle the house, just in case she's outside. The owners must be on holiday.'

They edged around the house, peering in through the windows—which was a fruitless exercise since nothing inside was really visible, but it made her feel better, as though every last possibility was being checked out.

'I *know* she's here,' Angela told him when they were back at the front. 'I feel it.'

'Mother's instinct coming to the fore after all these years? How touching.'

Angela felt a spurt of bitter tears come to her eyes. 'I'm not asking you to understand,' she said fiercely, 'I'm just asking you to believe me. I want to check the gardens. Will you help me or do I have to do it on my own?'

'I'll take the back,' he told her. 'There's a wood there that stretches down to the fields. You take the sides. There's quite a bit of ground to cover—two acres—so I'll meet you back here in fifteen minutes.'

He headed off and she branched away, calling and checking. After fifteen minutes she'd had no success.

Nor had he. There was something niggling at the back of her mind, though, as they made their way back to the car, and it was only when she was about to step in that it clicked. Outhouses. Away from the house and barely visible behind a row of conifers.

'Yes. The outhouses. I'd forgotten about those. How did you know?' he asked when she voiced her thoughts. She could feel the weight of his curiosity pressing down on her. It was waiting, she thought, for the opportunity to manifest itself in another round of scathing criticism.

'I told you,' she explained, 'your sister kept in touch. It was one of my stipulations when she adopted Natasha. There are two outhouses round the back. They used to be pigsties, of all things, but one of them was converted into useable space. Natasha had her fourth birthday party there. I know—I was sent photos.' Her voice had taken on a defensive tone, but he didn't comment.

They walked in silence through the gap in the trees, and there they were—the outhouses. Angela didn't know which had been converted. It turned out to be the first one, and, like the house, it was in complete darkness.

She felt her heart sink, but she pushed open the door anyway—an old-fashioned stable door, painted cream—switched on the light and there she was, huddled on a chair in the corner of the room.

They both saw her at precisely the same time, and she saw them, although her eyes were quickly averted from Angela and came to rest on Nick.

Angela found that she hadn't anticipated this far ahead. She had expected to find Natasha, but her imagination had not crossed the barrier between finding and actually explaining. Nick strode forward, kneeling down next to the child, and Angela lagged behind, knowing for the first time what it was to be unwanted because of who she was.

Natasha's head was pressed against Nick's neck, and

there were muffled sounds emerging which could have been speech or could have been crying.

When they both stood up she reached impulsively and touched Natasha's shoulder. Her hand was shrugged off. They walked slowly towards the car and Angela followed a little distance behind.

How was it that in all her mental scenarios, this one had never been played out? She had imagined not getting the job, not gaining her daughter's trust, being dismissed on whatever grounds. She realised now that she had forgotten to work out the most important scenario of all. What she would do if and when Natasha discovered her identity.

As the car sped back towards London she sat in the back seat, invisible, aching to explain but knowing that if she uttered a word the house of cards would collapse just a little bit more.

She had now been without sleep for nearly twenty-four hours, but she had never felt more wide awake in her life. She could barely see the top of Natasha's head over the car seat, but her eyes were glued to the dark hair, willing her to turn around, to say something—anything.

But they completed the drive in silence, and when they got to the house Nick, with his arms around his niece once again, nodded in the direction of the sitting room, where she went reluctantly, to stare at her watch, sitting on the very edge of a chair, not quite knowing what the next step in this nightmare was going to be.

It was over an hour before he returned.

Immediately she sprang out of the chair. 'Please. How is she?' Be as calm as you can, she told herself, but her voice emerged pleading and semi-coherent.

'She's had a shock.' He looked at her without the expected criticism then went across to the bar and poured himself a glass of mineral water.

'Have you explained…?'

'To the best of my ability, but she hasn't responded. She needs time to think things through.'

'May I go up and see her? Please?'

Nick looked at her for a long time over the rim of his glass, and finally he shook his head. 'I don't think that would be very wise,' he said, in the sort of gentle voice that said so much, that told her that he pitied her. 'She's upset and angry, and seeing you just now would probably make things worse.'

'Yes.' Her voice was listless and defeated. Her shoulders sagged. 'I never dreamed that things would end up like this,' she said, without looking at him. 'If I had had a crystal ball… Well, no good trying to climb back into the past and change it, is it? I know you won't believe me, but you have no idea what it felt like when I stopped hearing from your sister. It's been everything being here, being close to her, and I thought that she was beginning to trust me.'

She sighed. 'I knew that one day I would have to tell her the truth, and I honestly didn't envisage what I would say, but I believed it would have a happy ending.' She laughed bitterly and looked across at him. 'After everything I've been through, it's incredible to think that I could have been so naïve.'

'Hopeful might be a better word.'

'Hopeful, naïve…' She shrugged. 'It all comes down to the same thing in the end, doesn't it?' She stared vacantly in his direction and finally got up the courage to ask what had to be asked. 'So, what happens now?'

'This isn't going to be easy for you,' he said heavily,

cradling the glass in his hands. 'But I think the best thing for you to do is leave.'

Angela remained sitting quite still, feeling the colour drain from her face. She knew, very deep down, that he was being sensible, but the shock of it still made her tremble.

'Natasha needs time to think things over. When she has, I'm fairly certain that she'll want to contact you.'

'Yes.' The voice came out as drained of colour as her face was. When? she asked herself with a sickening sense of dread. When will she want to contact me? In a month's time? A year? Ever? 'I'll go upstairs and pack my things.'

'There's no need to do that. You can leave late in the morning.'

'No.' She stood up and smoothed her dress down, and realised that her hands were perspiring. 'No, I'd rather do it now, if you don't mind. I'll take a taxi back to my house. I don't think there'll be any trains running yet.'

'Don't be a fool. Take the car.'

'No, really, I'd rather not.' She managed a smile of sorts as she walked towards the door. As she passed him she paused and said carefully, 'You gave me the chance to get to know my daughter, for a while. Thank you for that. It meant a great deal to me.'

Noble sentiments and self-control didn't quite seem to go hand in hand, though, and she hurriedly walked out of the room before she made a fool of herself by bursting into tears in front of him.

Her packing was accomplished with maximum speed. Halfway through she phoned a taxi company and ordered a taxi, and was on her way back to her house within the hour. She hadn't dared take the risk of looking in on Natasha, just in case she wasn't asleep. Nor had she stopped to say goodbye to Nick. It would have hurt too much.

Within a fortnight she had settled back into a routine of sorts. Luckily, she had the cottage to herself, as Lesley was away for three weeks on a school trip. The school, to whom she had given the minimum of information, had agreed to take her back but she had another week or so before she started. Which was a stroke of luck because she needed, she realised, to sit by the phone, just in case it rang. She had even invested in an answering machine, to avoid the possibility of there being no reply when and if her daughter tried to get in touch.

She didn't. There was a trickle of messages from friends, who had heard, on the grapevine, that she had returned, and Angela returned their shows of friendliness with a desultory feeling of obligation, but her heart was not in it. She was playing a waiting game now, except she had no idea when the waiting would end, or even if it ever would. It was like being in a tunnel, desperately hoping that round the next corner there would be a flicker of light only to find ever more darkness ahead.

She was sitting in front of the television one night, thinking all the usual thoughts which never seemed to go away, when she heard a knock on the door. She almost ignored it. The light in the sitting room was not visible from the front door. She could simply slink into the darkness and wait until whoever it was got the message and left. When there was a further round of persistent knocking, however, she eventually heaved herself up, excuses at the ready, pulled open the door and then stood. Stood and stared and stared and stared, until Nick asked politely whether they might come in.

Natasha was holding his hand and her expression was

one of sullen wariness, just as it had been when Angela had first met her. She dragged her steps as Angela, overcome with nerves as she realised that yet another scenario had emerged for which she was utterly unprepared, ushered them into the sitting room.

'Uncle Nick made me come here,' Natasha said, and Nick threw her a dry smile and tugged her hair.

'Little liar,' he murmured softly, and Natasha blushed and looked fairly furious. 'I think I'll make myself some coffee,' he said, eyeing the direction of the kitchen, and Angela nodded vaguely, grateful for his tact.

As soon as he had left the room, Natasha, wringing her hands on her lap and still frowning mutinously, said, 'You lied to me! You left me! I hate you!'

And she burst into tears.

CHAPTER TEN

'How many cups of coffee have you had?' Angela pushed open the kitchen door and sat down at the table, a very small pine table which she had bought second-hand, complete with that mellow, well-worn look so popular now but not quite as popular at the time she had bought it.

It was an old-fashioned kitchen. No fitted cupboards, just a dresser and a couple of free-standing units which she had painted in a washed-out yellow to match the curtains, and no overhead fluorescent lighting.

She gave him a tired smile and rested her head momentarily on the back of her hand, then sat up and looked at him.

'Let's see,' he drawled, looking at his watch. 'I've been here for a little over an hour and a half. That makes three cups, according to my calculation.' He was perched against the dresser, but now he moved to sit opposite her, handing her a mug which she gratefully accepted, liking the warmth against the palms of her hands.

'Thank you for bringing her,' Angela said at last, and he shrugged.

'She wanted to come. I wasn't about to argue her out of it.'

'I waited and waited,' she murmured, gazing down into the creamy brown liquid. 'It was hard to hold onto hope.

I tried to put myself in her position...she was angry and confused and upset. But I've explained now.'

'How did she take it?'

'Did she discuss it with you after I'd gone?' She countered his question with one of her own.

'In fits and starts. But she missed you. I could see it on her face every time I looked at her.'

Angela smiled when she thought of that. How much had Natasha taken in of what she had said this evening? She had omitted some of the details, had painted the picture in broad terms that a child could understand.

'Thank you for staying in the kitchen,' she said eventually. 'I needed the time alone with her. She's asleep now. I put her to sleep in my bed.' The thought of that made her smile again, because bridges would have to be built—slowly, but they would be built, in time. She was sure of that.

'And you?' he asked, not quite meeting her eyes. 'Have you got a job as yet?'

'My old school has agreed to have me back. It was very good of them.' She paused awkwardly, not meeting his eyes either, and not knowing where to go from here.

Now that she was alone with him, she realised how much she remembered about the way he looked, the sound of his voice, the force of feeling which his presence aroused in her. What about you? she wanted to ask. Have *you* missed me? Have you thought of me at all? Do you still despise me?

'What happens next?' she asked. 'I know that you're Natasha's guardian, but...'

'You're her mother and you want her to live with you.'

'It's something that we need to discuss,' Angela told him, taking a deep breath and looking at him directly.

'I'm afraid I shall never be able to support her in the lifestyle that you could...'

'The money is immaterial.' He stood up abruptly and walked across to the kitchen sink. He stared out of the window, his back to her. 'Anyway, Natasha isn't exactly destitute. As a matter of fact, she has a great deal of money in trust for her—a legacy from Clive and Amanda.'

Angela hadn't thought of that, and it didn't make any difference anyway. She wanted her daughter with her and Natasha needed her.

'I suppose we should let the courts decide what happens...' she began hesitantly.

'I doubt there will be any obstacles,' he said, turning around to face her. 'The circumstances are extraordinary, but you are her natural mother, after all.' He paused and then said harshly, 'So, how does it feel to get what you wanted all along?'

'You make it sound as though it was all some kind of game. It wasn't.'

'But she was the reason you came, and the reason you stayed. In fact she was the reason for a lot of the things that you did, wasn't she?' When she didn't answer, he carried on, 'If Natasha does end up with you, perhaps you could see your way to according me visiting rights. For one thing, I happen to be very fond of her, and for another, I think it's important that she remembers her link with my sister.'

'Of course!' Angela's head shot up. 'And there's no need to use that aggressive tone with me!' She sighed and rested back in her chair with her eyes half shut. 'I don't want to argue with you.'

'Don't you? And what if I want to argue with *you*?'

Her eyes flew open and she looked at him, puzzled.

'Why on earth would you want to do that? I know that I deceived you, but it was never a...personal thing.'

He gave her a harsh frown, darkening, which made her suspect that she had probably said the wrong thing, so she lapsed into silence.

'Perhaps,' she ventured after a while, 'you could leave her here for the night and return for her in the morning?'

'And perhaps when I return in the morning, you'll have another reason for me to leave her for another night? The fact is, she has her school term to complete. Not to mention the little technicality of all her things in London.' He turned away and then said calmly, 'I have a proposition to make to you.'

Angela felt a swift rush of adrenaline through her, like a high-voltage current. 'What kind of proposition?'

'You could always marry me. That way you can be with her and her lifestyle need not be disrupted. She has friends at her school; she's only now beginning to find her feet there.'

'What?' She carefully put her mug on the table and held onto the table top, because everything suddenly seemed to be spinning wildly around her.

'You heard me.' His eyes were shuttered. 'It seems a sensible suggestion to me.'

'In that case, you must have taken leave of your senses,' Angela told him. She had a vivid image of life with him, sharing his bed every night, with the freedom to touch. Except he wasn't offering her love, was he? And the freedom to touch was very different from the freedom to express her feelings. Marriage without love, which was what he was offering her, was little more than a trap—or at least, she thought, it would be for her.

'I understand what you're saying about her schooling. But we can work around that—children adapt quite easily. She would settle into a new school with no problems.' The silence between them dragged on, like a piece of elastic pulled to its maximum stretching point.

'In other words, you find the idea loathsome, is that it?'

'I never said that! It's just that…'

'Just that what…?'

Angela didn't look at him. She stared down at the table, tracing a pattern on the top of her finger while her heart somersaulted inside her.

'Look,' she said evenly, 'I realise what you're saying, that Natasha's settled at school, but I have a great deal of experience with these things, and believe me when I tell you that if she comes here to live with me she won't have a problem in making new friends. Your solution to the problem is really a little drastic. Anyway, it's out of the question. I agree, though, that we shall have to sort something out for the remainder of her school term. If that's all right with you.'

She glanced at him and saw that his face was set in rigid lines. Why was he being difficult? She didn't want to dwell further on his proposal. If she thought too hard about that, she would have to tear herself away from the temptation of throwing caution to the winds and doing something which, she suspected, would not be the right thing. A clean break was for the best, even though it might hurt like hell to start with. Time would ease the pain of unrequited love, and she would have her daughter with her.

'And what would you suggest? Since, as you tell me, you have a great deal of experience in this field?'

'She could travel up to see me at weekends…'

'You could always move back down to London for the remaining weeks that she's at school.' His voice was challenging, and she looked at him, puzzled. 'I suppose,' he continued with the same odd aggression in his voice, 'you'll tell me that that's another drastic solution?'

'If it weren't for my circumstances here it would be a good idea, but—'

'And what are your circumstances here?' He interrupted her before she could finish the explanation. She kind of wished that he would sit down, so that she didn't have to crane her neck every time she spoke to him.

'I told you,' Angela explained evenly, 'I have a job, which, inconveniently, won't wait until the beginning of the new term. The girl I'm replacing is leaving to have a baby, so she can't finish the term out. If I don't take this opportunity I'm not sure when another chance will arise. Teaching jobs aren't that easy to come by, and...'

'Are you sure that's the only reason that you're so damned set on staying here? London is full of teaching jobs. You could always get one there, and then Natasha could remain where she was.'

'Why are you so keen for me to be in London?' she asked, worriedly hoping that he wasn't about to go back on his word and try and fight her for custody of her daughter. She might be Natasha's natural mother, true enough, but she had no idea how the courts would view her, especially when the legal guardian was a man like Nick—rich, powerful, influential. Was this all some sort of prelude to something more sinister? It didn't make sense, but then neither did his attitude.

'You haven't answered my question,' he replied tersely, not quite meeting her eyes but still managing to radiate a feeling of threat. 'Is the job the only reason that you're so keen to remain here?'

'Why else?' She frowned and tried to sift through what

he was saying in an attempt to deduce some meaning which was eluding her.

'You tell me. I mean, you lied your way into my house. What else have you lied about? Is there some man up here, waiting in the wings for you to return? Some man whose presence might have jeopardised your little game plan?'

'That's an awful thing to say!'

'But,' he said harshly, advancing towards her, which, given the dimensions of her kitchen, only necessitated a couple of steps forward, 'is it the truth?'

Angela looked up at him, which made the muscles in her neck ache, although she was almost more alarmed when he decided to sit down—not in the chair facing her, with the protection of the table in between them, but in the chair next to hers, so that they were now heart-stoppingly close to one another. Their knees were inches apart and his presence, overwhelming as it had been before, now threatened to engulf her completely.

'Why on earth should it matter whether there's a man in my life or not?' she threw at him, staving off attack with the first line of defence that came to hand.

'Just answer me!'

'I'm only keen to stay here because of the job! Satisfied?'

'No!'

She waited for him to elaborate on this extraordinary monosyllable, but he didn't, and they stared at each other in an atmosphere thick with words unspoken. She could feel her heart pounding inside her, making her body rigid with tension and sending little prickles of awareness shooting through her.

'I'm afraid I can't let you stay up here.' His voice was strange, but she wasn't concentrating on the tenor of his voice. She was too busy trying to understand what he was talking about. Was this about Natasha? What else could it be?

'What do you mean, you can't let me stay here? What do you intend to do? Drag me down to London? Or maybe you could arrange a job in a school for me?' She gave a short, mirthless laugh.

'Why won't you marry me?'

The abruptness of the question took her by surprise and she looked at him, wide-eyed, for a few seconds, then felt colour creep into her cheeks. Because, she wanted to say, I'm in love with you. Isn't that the strangest reason in the world?

Since she had no intention of saying that, she remained silent, prepared to sit in silence until the cows came home, if need be.

'This is difficult for me to say,' he told her roughly, accusingly. 'No one likes to feel that they have been used...'

'I told you...'

'Just hear me out, would you?' But for a while he seemed uncertain as to which way the conversation should go. 'I went a little mad when I found out about you and Natasha. Like I said, I always suspected that you had an ulterior motive in putting yourself forward for what was, in effect, a non-existent job, but it never occurred to me that that was the reason. All of a sudden lots of things seemed to make sense, in a way that I didn't like at all.'

'I'm sorry...' Angela began, trailing off into silence.

'I especially didn't like it because...' He seemed to have some difficulty here, because he averted his face and looked like someone searching for the right words and not really having a great deal of success. 'The fact is…it seems that the house is empty without you in it.'

Angela felt a rush of pleasure, and for once there were no accompanying warning bells to make it subside. It stayed with her, filling her like a drug, making her heady and disorientated. She was sure that if he glanced at her face he would read everything there that she had tried so hard to conceal, but he wasn't looking at her at all. His eyes were focused in the general direction of the kitchen sink.

'It appears,' he continued, 'that I've become accustomed to you.'

'You've become accustomed to me?' she asked, with enough of a smile in her voice to make him finally look at her.

'I'm so glad that you find this amusing.' He frowned and glared at her, but there was a certain vulnerability in his discomfort that made her smile more. 'Would you like me to carry on? Or would you rather just sit there grinning like a Cheshire cat?'

'I'd like you to carry on,' she murmured quietly, re-arranging her smile into something suitably serious, even though her heart was now doing cartwheels inside her. 'Very much.'

'After I recovered from my anger, I thought that wounded pride would make me forget about you. I decided that the best thing you ever did was leave and that the day I set eyes on you again would be a day too soon.' He sighed and shook his head, then he took her fingers in his hands and examined them, turning them over as though fascinated with a light touch that was as deadly to her self-composure as an out and out advance. 'I made up my mind that there were lots of other women in the world. You weren't the only one. But somehow I couldn't get up the energy to ask any of those women out. The thought of it made my stomach churn.'

'Did it?' she asked softly, closing her fingers around his.

'Which brings me right back to where I started. I discovered something in your absence. I missed you. However much I told myself that I disliked you for what you had done, that you had taken me for a fool, that I was well rid of you, I still missed you like hell. I have never felt as powerless as I have done over the past two weeks since you left. It seems,' he said heavily, 'that I need you, and I need you because somehow, without me looking, I've managed to fall in love with you.'

She had known that, had seen the admission in the defensive set of his face and heard it in the struggle of his words, but her heart still soared when he finally admitted it, used the words she had longed to hear. She could have shouted her joy to the heavens. She wanted the whole world to know.

'I realise that I haven't exactly been a gem of thoughtful understanding with you from the word go, but I love you, Angela, and I can't let you go. I won't let you slip out of my life, even if I have to fight you to make you see things that way.'

'There'll be no need for that,' she told him in a low voice, and their eyes met. 'I hate fights.' She smiled at him. 'Especially when they're not necessary.'

She leaned forward, placing both her hands on his thighs, and kissed his mouth in a slow, lingering kiss that tasted of honey and made her bones feel as though they were melting.

'You have no idea how I've waited to hear you say those words,' she said, breaking away from him but holding his head with both her hands. 'I never imagined that

I would fall in love with you, and I never, ever imagined that you could ever fall in love with me. I made love to you because I wanted you, so badly, but then I realised that I would have to walk away because…' She sighed. 'Because I thought that you would get bored with me very quickly and want me out of your house, out of your life, and then I would lose my daughter for the second time.'

'You love me,' was all he said, although he was grinning. 'You should have said. Saved me my admission.'

'Saved you your admission? I enjoyed every minute of it! I only wish I'd captured it on tape so that I could replay it on a daily basis!'

'You witch!' But he laughed and pulled her to him, so that she was sitting on his lap, legs straddling his, arms loosely around his neck. He undid the buttons of her blouse, one by one, and eased it off, followed by her bra, then he cupped her breasts in his hands.

'Have you ever made love in a kitchen before?' he asked casually, and she gave a low-throated laugh.

'Never. But there's a first time for everything, wouldn't you say?'

His eyes darkened with desire. 'Definitely.'

A first time for everything, she thought. Even happiness.

Don't miss a fabulous new trilogy
from a rising star in

 HARLEQUIN PRESENTS®

KIM LAWRENCE

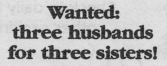 TRIPLET BRIDES

**Wanted:
three husbands
for three sisters!**

*Triplet sisters—they're
the best, the closest,
of friends…*

Meet lively, spirited Anna in
Wild and Willing!, Harlequin Presents® #2078
On sale December 1999

Lindy meets the man of her dreams in
The Secret Father, Harlequin Presents® #2096
On sale March 2000

Hope's story is the thrilling conclusion
to this fabulous trilogy in
An Innocent Affair, Harlequin Presents® #2114
On sale June 2000

Available wherever Harlequin books are sold.

 HARLEQUIN®
Makes any time special ™

Visit us at www.romance.net   HPTB1

HARLEQUIN PRESENTS®

SWEET REVENGE ~~Seduction~~

They wanted to get even. Instead they got...married!

by bestselling author

Penny Jordan

Don't miss Penny Jordan's latest enthralling miniseries about four special women. Kelly, Anna, Beth and Dee share a bond of friendship and a burning desire to avenge a wrong. But in their quest for revenge, they each discover an even stronger emotion.
Love.

Look out for all four books in Harlequin Presents®:

November 1999
THE MISTRESS ASSIGNMENT

December 1999
LOVER BY DECEPTION

January 2000
A TREACHEROUS SEDUCTION

February 2000
THE MARRIAGE RESOLUTION

Available at your favorite retail outlet.

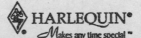

HARLEQUIN®
Makes any time special ™

London's streets aren't just paved with gold—they're home to three of the world's most eligible bachelors!

You can meet these gorgeous men, and the women who steal their hearts, in:

NOTTING HILL GROOMS

Look out for these tantalizing romances set in London's exclusive Notting Hill, written by highly acclaimed authors who, between them, have sold more than 35 million books worldwide!

Irresistible Temptation by Sara Craven
Harlequin Presents® #2077
On sale December 1999

Reform of the Playboy by Mary Lyons
Harlequin Presents® #2083
On sale January 2000

The Millionaire Affair by Sophie Weston
Harlequin Presents® #2089
On sale February 2000

Available wherever Harlequin books are sold.

HARLEQUIN®
Makes any time special ™

HPNHG